The Weaver of Worlds:

Knitting a Kingdom's Fate

This book is a work of fiction. While the character and their journey were inspired by the spirit and creativity of a real individuals, the story, characters, and events contained within are entirely products of imagination and are not based on real life. This narrative was created with the assistance of artificial intelligence.

By Richard Dell Schwarz

Copyright © 2025 Richard Dell Schwarz

Foreword

Mia,

As you turn the pages of this story, "The Weaver of Worlds," I hope you find a piece of yourself within its magic. This isn't just a tale of adventure; it's a whisper from my heart, a testament to the incredible spirit I see in you every day.

You've always had a special way of looking at the world, a knack for seeing beauty and a quiet strength. This story reminds me of that light. It's a reminder that true power lies not in grand gestures, but in the quiet, steady work of creation, mending, and connection. Just like the Mia in these pages, you have the ability to weave wonders, bringing warmth and hope to those around you.

With all my love,

Dad-Dad

Table of Contents

Chapter 1: A Stitch in Time, A New Place

The last U-Haul box, optimistically labeled "Kitchen - Misc. Chaos," finally thudded onto the scuffed linoleum of their new Newark, Arkansas kitchen. Mia Martinez, dust motes dancing in the late afternoon sunbeams that slanted through the grimy window, wiped a smear of grime from her forehead with the back of a gloved hand. Her early twenties felt less like a vibrant beginning and more like a never-ending series of packing and unpacking. Boerne, Texas, with its rolling hills, familiar faces, and the comforting scent of cedar, felt a million miles and a lifetime away.

Ethan Morgan, her boyfriend of five years, a man whose easygoing charm could diffuse almost any crisis, let out a triumphant groan from the living room. "That's it, babe! Last one! We're officially residents of the great state of Arkansas!" His voice, usually a warm baritone, was raspy with exertion and the lingering dust of their cross-country trek.

Mia managed a weak smile. "Hooray for us," she mumbled, surveying the kitchen. It was a relic of a bygone era, all avocado green countertops and chipped white cabinets. The house itself was a modest, two-bedroom ranch, perched on a quiet street with a sprawling, slightly overgrown backyard. It was a far cry from the quaint, modern apartment they'd shared in Boerne, but it was theirs. Or, rather, it was Ethan's. His new job as a junior engineer at a manufacturing plant just outside of town had necessitated the move, a leap of faith they'd both agreed to, though Mia's internal compass still spun wildly, searching for true north.

Pinto Bean, or just Bean, a scruffy terrier mix with ears that flopped at jaunty angles and eyes that held the wisdom of a thousand belly rubs, padded into the kitchen. She sniffed at the "Misc. Chaos" box with a discerning nose, then looked up at Mia, a silent question in her gaze. *Are we done yet? Can we play?*

"Almost, sweet pea," Mia murmured, scratching behind Bean's ears. The dog leaned into her touch, a low rumble of contentment vibrating in her chest. Bear, their other canine companion, a lumbering, shaggy golden retriever with a heart as golden as his fur, was already sprawled out in the living room, a furry, exhausted rug amidst a sea of cardboard. He'd taken the move harder than Bean, his usual boisterous energy replaced by a resigned sigh every time another box was loaded or unloaded.

Mia peeled off her work gloves, revealing hands that, despite the day's labor, still held the delicate calluses of a knitter. Her fingers, long and nimble, were accustomed to the rhythmic dance of needles and yarn, not the abrasive grip of packing tape. She missed her knitting. She missed the quiet hum of creation, the way a skein of yarn transformed under her touch into something tangible, something beautiful.

The past few weeks had been a blur of logistics. Selling their old furniture, saying tearful goodbyes to friends and family, the endless drive across state lines, the dizzying array of new streets and unfamiliar landmarks. Newark was small, a town that seemed to breathe at a slower pace than Boerne. The air here felt different, thicker, carrying the scent of damp earth and distant fields rather than the dry, dusty aroma of Texas. It wasn't bad, not exactly. Just… different. And different, for Mia, often translated to unsettling.

Ethan reappeared, wiping his brow with the back of his hand. His dark hair was disheveled, and his usually vibrant blue eyes were shadowed with fatigue, but a genuine smile lit his face. "Alright, that's the last of the heavy lifting for today. What do you say we order some pizza and collapse?"

"Sounds like the best idea you've had all day," Mia agreed, pushing a stray strand of brown hair out of her eyes. She felt a pang of guilt. Ethan had been so excited about this opportunity, so supportive of her own freelance graphic design work, even though it meant she could technically work from anywhere. He deserved her enthusiasm, not her quiet melancholy.

As Ethan called in their order, Mia wandered into what would be her studio — a small, sunlit room off the living area. It was still packed to the gills with boxes, but one, clearly labeled "Mia's Happy Place," stood out. She knelt, her fingers tracing the familiar scrawl. Inside, nestled amongst tissue paper, were her knitting needles. Not just any needles, but *her* needles. The ones her grandmother had given her years ago, a beautiful set of polished rosewood, smooth and warm beneath her fingertips. They weren't particularly old, but they felt ancient, imbued with a quiet history.

She pulled out a pair, the largest size, perfect for chunky blankets. As her fingers closed around the wood, a faint, almost imperceptible warmth spread through her palm. It wasn't the warmth of friction or residual heat; it felt internal, as if the wood itself held a tiny, sleeping ember. She frowned, turning the needle over in her hand. Had she imagined it? The house was old, maybe the air currents were playing tricks. She dismissed it, placing the needles back in their case. The thought, however, lingered, a tiny, persistent hum at the back of her mind.

Dinner arrived, a greasy, glorious pepperoni pizza that tasted like victory after a day of manual labor. They ate on the floor, surrounded by boxes, the dogs curled up contentedly at their feet, occasionally nudging them for a dropped crust. Ethan recounted his first day at the plant, the new colleagues, the complex machinery. He was clearly energized, his passion for engineering shining through his tired demeanor.

Mia listened, offering encouraging hums and questions, but her mind kept drifting. She thought about her grandmother, the woman who had taught her to knit, whose hands had moved with such grace and purpose, weaving stories into every stitch. Her grandmother had always said knitting was more than just a hobby; it was a way to connect, to create, to bring comfort and beauty into the world. Mia had always taken it literally, but now, a strange new possibility flickered.

The next few days settled into a routine of sorts. Ethan left early for work, and Mia tackled the

unpacking, box by tedious box. She found her
rhythm in organizing, in transforming the chaotic
piles into something resembling a home. She hung
curtains, arranged books on makeshift shelves, and
tried to infuse the old house with their own
personality.

But the quiet longing for Boerne persisted. She
missed her weekly coffee dates with her best friend,
the familiar trails she used to hike with Bean and
Bear, the comfort of knowing every shortcut and
every back road. Newark felt foreign, a place she was
observing rather than truly inhabiting.

It was during one of these quiet, reflective moments
that Mia decided to knit. She needed the comfort,
the familiar rhythm, the sense of creating something
new in a world that felt overwhelmingly new and old
at the same time. She retrieved her rosewood needles
and a skein of soft, sky-blue yarn – a gift from
Ethan, chosen for its calming hue.

She decided to knit a small, whimsical rabbit for
Bean. Bean loved soft things, and a knitted friend
seemed like the perfect welcome gift to their new,
strange home. Mia settled onto the worn armchair in
the living room, Bean immediately curling up at her
feet, Bear sighing dramatically as he flopped down
beside her. The afternoon sun, now a brilliant gold,

streamed through the window, illuminating the dust motes and the quiet concentration on Mia's face.

As she cast on, the rosewood needles felt different. Not just warm, but almost… alive. A subtle vibration hummed beneath her fingertips, a faint thrumming that resonated with the gentle click of the needles. She dismissed it as her imagination, a trick of tired nerves, but the feeling was undeniably there. It was like holding a tuning fork that had just been struck, a faint, lingering resonance.

She worked steadily, her fingers moving with practiced ease. The yarn flowed smoothly, each stitch a tiny act of creation. She focused on the simple beauty of the craft, the way the loops formed a fabric, the way the rabbit's shape began to emerge from the formless skein. She thought of Bean, her floppy ears, her curious nose, her endless capacity for joy. She poured all her affection into the tiny stitches.

Hours passed, marked only by the shifting sunlight and the occasional snore from Bear. The rabbit took shape, its little body plump and soft, its ears perked, its tiny tail a fluffy puff. Mia knitted two small black beads for eyes, and a pink thread for its nose. She was meticulous, wanting it to be perfect for Bean.

Finally, she tied off the last knot, snipping the yarn with a small pair of scissors. The rabbit was complete, a charming, palm-sized creature. Mia held it up, admiring her handiwork. It was perhaps the cutest little rabbit she'd ever made.

She lowered it, intending to place it gently on Bean's head, but before it even touched the dog's fur, something extraordinary happened.

The rabbit twitched.

Not a subtle twitch, not a trick of the light, but a distinct, undeniable twitch. Its button eyes, which Mia had just sewn on, blinked. Then, slowly, deliberately, its tiny knitted head turned, its gaze sweeping across the room, as if taking in its surroundings for the very first time.

Mia froze, her breath catching in her throat. Her mind scrambled for an explanation. A draft? A trick of her tired eyes? But the rabbit moved again, its little nose twitching, its knitted ears wiggling.

Then, with a soft, almost imperceptible rustle, it hopped.

It hopped off her lap, landing softly on the rug beside Bean. Bean, who had been dozing, lifted her head, her own ears perking up. She sniffed the knitted rabbit, then let out a surprised little yip, her tail giving a tentative wag. Bear, roused by the commotion, lifted his massive head, his eyes blinking slowly, trying to comprehend the small, animated creature now sitting upright on the floor.

The rabbit looked at Bean, then at Bear, then back at Mia, its button eyes wide with what could only be described as curiosity. It took another hop, a small, tentative movement, then another, exploring the unfamiliar landscape of the living room rug.

Mia stared, her jaw slack. This wasn't a trick. This wasn't imagination. This was… impossible. But it was happening. Right there, in front of her, a knitted rabbit was alive.

A wave of disbelief washed over her, followed quickly by a surge of pure, unadulterated wonder. Her heart hammered in her chest, a frantic drumbeat against her ribs. She reached out a trembling hand, slowly, cautiously, towards the hopping rabbit. It paused, its head tilted, watching her. When her finger gently brushed its soft, yarn fur, it felt warm, almost like a tiny, living creature.

"Ethan," she whispered, her voice barely a breath. "Ethan!"

He was still at work, of course. She was alone with her impossible creation.

She spent the rest of the afternoon in a state of bewildered fascination. The rabbit, after its initial exploration, seemed content to hop around the living room, occasionally nudging Bean with its nose or attempting to climb Bear's massive paw. It was undeniably alive, a tiny, knitted miracle.

When Ethan finally came home, tired but smiling, Mia practically tackled him at the door. "You are not going to believe what happened!" she exclaimed, dragging him into the living room.

He looked around, confused. "What? Did the fridge finally give up the ghost?"

"No! Look!" Mia pointed to the knitted rabbit, which was currently attempting to chew on the corner of a throw pillow.

Ethan blinked. He walked over, picked up the rabbit, and turned it over in his hands. "It's a rabbit, babe. A really cute one. Did you just finish it?"

"No, Ethan, it's *alive*," Mia insisted, her voice rising with a mixture of excitement and exasperation. "It hopped off my lap! It blinked! It's moving right now!"

Ethan chuckled, a low, rumbling sound. "You've been unpacking too long, sweetie. You're seeing things." He set the rabbit down.

As if on cue, the rabbit hopped. It took two distinct, undeniable hops across the rug.

Ethan's smile faltered. He blinked again, then leaned closer, his brow furrowed in confusion. "Did that just… hop?"

"Yes!" Mia practically shouted. "I told you!"

He picked up the rabbit again, examining it closely. He poked its nose, its ears. It twitched. Its button eyes blinked.

"Okay," Ethan said slowly, his voice a mixture of awe and disbelief. "Okay, so… you knitted a living rabbit."

"I guess so!" Mia felt a giddy laugh bubble up inside her. "It's my needles! They felt weird while I was knitting it. Warm. Like they had a little hum."

They spent the evening in a state of delighted bewilderment, observing the knitted rabbit. It was a docile creature, content to explore the floor, occasionally nuzzling their ankles. Bean and Bear, after their initial surprise, seemed to accept it as a new, albeit unusual, member of the pack.

The next morning, Mia, still buzzing with excitement, decided to experiment. She pulled out a skein of deep emerald green yarn and her rosewood needles. She decided to knit a simple scarf, something quick, to test the other ability she'd vaguely perceived.

As she knitted, the familiar warmth and subtle hum returned to the needles, stronger this time, almost a gentle vibration. She finished the scarf quickly, a soft, ordinary-looking piece of knitted fabric. She held it up.

"Okay, magic scarf, do your thing," she whispered, half-joking.

And then, it shimmered.

The emerald green fabric rippled, not like light on water, but as if it's very fibers were shifting. The soft, woolly texture seemed to smooth, to become impossibly fine, and the color deepened, taking on the lustrous sheen of raw silk. Mia gasped. She ran her fingers over it; it felt cool and smooth, exactly like silk.

"Whoa," Ethan said, having just walked into the room, coffee mug in hand. "What did you do to that scarf?"

"Watch this," Mia said, her eyes wide with wonder. She focused, imagining rough burlap. The scarf shimmered again, the silk-like sheen vanishing, replaced by the coarse, nubby texture and dull, earthy tone of burlap. She rubbed it between her fingers; it felt exactly like burlap.

"It can change!" she exclaimed. "It can look like anything! Feel like anything!"

Over the next few days, Mia experimented relentlessly. She knitted a small, intricate butterfly, and it fluttered around the room, its knitted wings beating silently. She made a tiny mouse, and it scurried across the floor with surprising speed. Each creation, no matter how small or simple, came to life.

And the clothes she made… they were truly extraordinary. A simple knitted dress could transform into a flowing gown of shimmering satin, then a sleek, modern jumpsuit, then a rustic peasant dress. The possibilities were endless. The disguises she could create were perfect, seamless, utterly convincing. The magic was real, and it was undeniably in her hands, channeled through her beloved rosewood needles.

The subtle hum of the needles became a comforting presence, a constant reminder of the extraordinary power she now wielded. It was a power that felt ancient, yet intimately connected to her, to her passion for knitting, to the quiet comfort it had always brought her.

But as the days turned into weeks, and Mia continued to explore her newfound abilities, strange occurrences began to manifest beyond the confines of their little house. Small, inexplicable things at first. A patch of wildflowers in their backyard, usually a riot of color, suddenly glowed with an ethereal light at dusk. The old oak tree down the street seemed to grow new, unusually vibrant leaves overnight. Whispers started circulating among the locals – hushed tales of odd lights in the sky, of strange, melodious sounds carried on the wind, of animals behaving unusually.

"Did you hear about Mrs. Henderson's prize-winning pumpkin?" Ethan asked one evening, scrolling through his phone. "She swears it grew to twice its size overnight, and it's glowing."

Mia paused, her knitting needles still. "Glowing?"

"Yeah, like, actually glowing. She thinks it's some kind of new fertilizer, but everyone else thinks it's… well, they don't know what they think." He chuckled, but there was a hint of unease in his voice.

Mia had a feeling. A growing, unsettling feeling that these strange occurrences weren't isolated incidents. They felt connected, somehow, to the magic that now pulsed through her needles. It was as if the veil between their world and another was thinning, becoming porous, allowing something extraordinary to seep through.

One Saturday, Mia decided to brave the local farmer's market. She needed fresh produce, and perhaps a distraction from the growing sense of unease. The market was a bustling hub of activity, filled with the scent of fresh bread, ripe berries, and earthy vegetables. As she browsed a stall of homemade jams, an old woman with eyes like polished river stones and a cascade of silver hair caught her attention.

The woman was selling intricate, hand-woven baskets, each one a work of art. Her face was a roadmap of wrinkles, etched with a lifetime of stories. She looked up as Mia approached, a knowing glint in her ancient eyes.

"Lovely day for a market, isn't it, dearie?" the old woman rasped, her voice surprisingly strong.

"It is," Mia replied, admiring a particularly beautiful basket.

"You have hands that know how to weave," the woman said, her gaze fixed on Mia's fingers. "Hands that know the language of thread."

Mia felt a jolt. "I knit," she corrected, a little defensively.

The woman merely smiled, a slow, enigmatic curve of her lips. "Weaving, knitting, crocheting... all the same, in the grand tapestry. You feel it, don't you? The thinning of the veil."

Mia's heart skipped a beat. "The... thinning veil?"

"Aye," the woman nodded, her gaze drifting to the distant horizon. "The world is restless. A queen in a tower, a shadow of scales, a land in peril. It needs a Weaver of Light. Someone to mend what's broken."

Mia stared at her, a chill running down her spine. "What are you talking about?"

The old woman leaned closer, her voice dropping to a conspiratorial whisper. "Solara. A land of magic, now shrouded in gloom. Its benevolent ruler, Queen Sasha, imprisoned by a mighty dragon, Dreadwing, who serves a dark sorcerer. The balance is broken, child. The threads are frayed."

Mia felt an inexplicable pull towards these tales, a strange sense of recognition. It was as if the old woman was speaking of something she already knew, deep in her bones. "How do you know this?"

The woman simply tapped her temple. "Some things are known, not learned. The land cries out. And you, with your hands that weave light, you are meant to hear it." She pressed a small, intricately carved wooden charm into Mia's hand. "When the time is right, the path will reveal itself. Follow the threads, Weaver."

Before Mia could ask another question, the old woman turned, her silver hair shimmering in the sunlight, and melted into the bustling crowd, as if she were never there at all. Mia stood there, the wooden charm warm in her palm, her mind reeling. Solara. Queen Sasha. A dragon. A dark sorcerer. It sounded like something out of a fairy tale, yet the old woman's words had resonated with an unsettling truth.

She hurried home, her head spinning. She found Ethan in the living room, attempting to assemble a notoriously difficult flat-pack bookshelf.

"Ethan," she began, her voice urgent, "I just had the strangest conversation at the market." She recounted the old woman's words, the tales of Solara, Queen Sasha, and the dragon Dreadwing.

Ethan, usually so grounded, listened intently, his screwdriver forgotten in his hand. When she finished, he was silent for a long moment. "A queen in a tower? A dragon? Mia, are you sure you didn't just meet a very imaginative storyteller?"

"It wasn't like that," Mia insisted. "She knew about my hands. She knew about… the thinning veil. And the way she spoke, it felt real. Like she was telling me something important." She held out the wooden charm. "She gave me this."

Ethan took the charm, turning it over in his fingers. It was smooth, cool, and carved with what looked like a stylized tree, its branches intertwined with what could be threads. "It's beautiful," he admitted, "but…"

"And the glowing pumpkin," Mia interrupted. "And the weird lights. It's all connected, Ethan. I feel it. This magic, it's not just for making cute animals. It's… bigger." She looked at her rosewood needles, lying on the coffee table, catching the light. They seemed to pulse faintly, almost imperceptibly.

Ethan looked from the charm to Mia, then to the needles. He was a man of logic, of science, of tangible facts. But he had seen the knitted rabbit hop. He had seen the scarf change its texture and color. He couldn't deny what his own eyes had witnessed.

"So," he said slowly, "you think… you think there's a real place called Solara, and a real queen named Sasha, and a real dragon named Dreadwing?"

"I don't know what to think," Mia admitted, running a hand through her hair. "But what if? What if this magic, what if *my* magic, is for a reason? What if I'm supposed to help?"

Ethan walked over to her, pulling her into a comforting hug. He knew her, knew her kind heart, her unwavering sense of right and wrong. He knew that when Mia felt a pull, it was usually for a good reason.

"Okay," he said, his voice firm, his arms tightening around her. "Okay. Let's find out. Let's research this Solara. Let's see if there's anything, anything at all, that points to this being real."

Mia pulled back, her eyes shining with a mixture of fear and excitement. "Really? You'd do that?"

"Of course, I would," Ethan said, a small smile playing on his lips. "You found magical knitting needles, Mia. I think we're officially past the point of 'normal.' Besides," he added, a mischievous glint in his eye, "a quest sounds a lot more interesting than assembling this bookshelf."

And so, their quiet life in Newark, Arkansas, began to unravel, replaced by a growing sense of destiny. The boxes remained, some still unpacked, but their focus shifted. They spent hours poring over old books from the local library, searching online for obscure folklore, and even visiting the small, dusty historical society in town. They looked for any mention of Solara, of Queen Sasha, of dragons named Dreadwing, or of "Weavers of Light."

Most of their searches yielded nothing but dusty myths and fantastical tales. But then, late one night, huddled over Ethan's laptop, they stumbled upon an old, forgotten text digitized by a small, independent historical archive. It was a collection of ancient legends from a forgotten corner of Europe, and buried within its pages, a faint, almost illegible passage spoke of a land known as Solara, a place where magic flowed like rivers, and where a benevolent queen ruled from a shimmering castle. The text described Solara's reliance on a "Heart Weaver" to maintain its balance, a person whose craft could mend the very fabric of reality.

The passage was vague, almost poetic, but it was enough. It spoke of a time when the land was plunged into darkness by a "Shadow of Scales" and its queen imprisoned. It hinted at a hidden gateway, a portal that would only reveal itself to those with a "true heart and a weaver's touch."

Mia's breath hitched. "A Heart Weaver," she whispered, looking at her hands, then at her rosewood needles. "It's me. It has to be me."

Ethan, though still daunted by the sheer impossibility of it all, felt a surge of conviction. He had seen the magic. He had heard the old woman's words. And now, this ancient text, speaking of a "Heart Weaver" and a land in peril. It was too much to be coincidence.

He looked at Mia, her face illuminated by the glow of the laptop screen, her eyes wide with a mixture of fear and determination. He knew this was bigger than them, bigger than Newark, bigger than anything they had ever imagined.

"Okay," he said, his voice steady, his resolve hardening. "If you're the Heart Weaver, then I'm your… your loyal assistant. Your yarn-holder. Whatever you need." He squeezed her hand. "We'll figure this out. Together."

Mia smiled, a genuine, radiant smile that reached her eyes. The quiet longing for Boerne didn't vanish entirely, but it was overshadowed by a new, exhilarating sense of purpose. The world, which had felt so small and ordinary just weeks ago, had suddenly expanded, revealing hidden depths and unimaginable possibilities.

The mundane had given way to the magical. Their new home in Newark, Arkansas, was no longer just a house; it was a launching pad. And Mia Martinez, the girl who liked to knit, was about to discover that her needles were not just tools for creation, but keys to another world, a world that desperately needed her unique gift. The quest had unraveled, and they were ready to follow the threads, wherever they might lead. Even if it meant facing a mighty dragon.

Chapter 2: Threads of Wonder

The knitted rabbit, now affectionately named "Hopsy" by Ethan, was no longer a bewildering anomaly but a delightful, if utterly inexplicable, member of their household. It hopped, it twitched its nose, it even seemed to chase sunbeams across the living room floor with an uncanny, almost sentient curiosity. Bean, after her initial surprise, had adopted Hopsy as a curious, silent playmate, nudging it gently with her nose, bringing it her favorite squeaky toy, and sometimes just resting her head near it, watching its tiny, animated movements with a quiet fascination. Bear, ever the gentle giant, simply observed Hopsy with a calm, almost paternal gaze, occasionally offering a low, rumbling sigh that sounded remarkably like approval, as if he understood the profound strangeness of their new reality.

Mia, however, was still reeling. The sheer impossibility of it all hummed beneath her skin, a constant, exhilarating current that left her both breathless and energized. She'd spent the entire morning after Hopsy's animation in a state of restless energy, unable to focus on unpacking or her freelance graphic design work. Her gaze kept drifting to the rosewood needles, lying innocently on the coffee table, yet now imbued with an undeniable aura of mystery and latent power. They no longer seemed like mere tools; they felt like conduits.

"You really think it's the needles?" Ethan had asked over breakfast, stirring his coffee slowly, his expression a mixture of fascination and lingering skepticism. He was a man who thrived on logic, on cause and effect, on verifiable data. A living knitted rabbit defied every principle he understood, every scientific law he'd ever learned. He'd poked Hopsy, prodded it, even tried to find a hidden mechanism, but found nothing. It was simply… alive.

"What else could it be?" Mia countered, pushing a piece of toast around her plate, her appetite momentarily forgotten in the face of such profound wonder. "They felt warm. They hummed. And then… Hopsy." She gestured vaguely towards the living room where Hopsy was currently attempting to scale the leg of the armchair, its tiny knitted paws scrabbling adorably against the fabric, its button eyes fixed on some unseen summit.

Ethan conceded with a shrug, a slow, hesitant smile spreading across his face. "Fair point. So, what's next? Are you going to knit us a dragon for the backyard? Maybe a self-folding laundry basket?" He tried to keep his tone light, but Mia could hear the tremor of genuine wonder beneath it, the barely suppressed excitement. His logical mind was still struggling, but his adventurous spirit was clearly intrigued.

Mia's eyes widened at the suggestion of a dragon. "A dragon? Ethan, I don't even know what I'm doing! This is… accidental magic, if it's magic at all. I just knitted a rabbit." But the idea, once planted, began to take root in her mind, blossoming with impossible possibilities. If a simple rabbit could come to life, what else was possible? What were the limits of this power? The thought was both thrilling and terrifying.

Later that day, armed with a fresh skein of deep emerald green yarn – a luxurious merino wool that felt impossibly soft against her skin – and a renewed sense of purpose, Mia decided to experiment. She chose a simple project: a scarf. Something quick, something she could finish in an hour or two, to test the other strange sensation she'd experienced with the needles – the subtle shimmer, the fleeting impression that the fabric could change its very essence. She needed to understand the scope of this magic, to categorize it, to see if it was a one-off miracle or a repeatable phenomenon.

She settled into her favorite armchair, the one with the worn armrests that felt like an old friend, a comforting anchor in her rapidly changing reality. Bean immediately curled up at her feet, her soft fur a warm weight against Mia's ankles. Bear, sensing Mia's quiet focus, settled nearby with a contented sigh, his massive head resting on his paws, his eyes fixed on Mia's hands. The afternoon sun, now a brilliant gold, streamed through the window, illuminating the dust motes dancing in the air and the quiet, intense concentration on Mia's face.

As she cast on, the rosewood needles felt different again. Not just warm, but almost *vibrating* with an internal energy. A subtle hum resonated beneath her fingertips, a faint thrumming that was no longer ignorable, but a distinct, almost melodic pulse that resonated deep within her bones, a feeling that seemed to echo the very rhythm of her heartbeat. It was like holding a tuning fork that had just been struck, a faint, lingering resonance that settled deep in her soul. She didn't dismiss it this time. She embraced it, allowing the strange energy to flow through her fingers, into the yarn, guiding each stitch with an almost instinctive understanding.

She worked steadily, her fingers moving with practiced ease, each stitch a tiny act of creation, a deliberate weaving of intent into fiber. The emerald green yarn flowed smoothly, transforming under her touch into a soft, ordinary-looking piece of knitted fabric. She focused on the simple beauty of the craft, the way the loops formed a cohesive whole, the way the scarf's shape began to emerge from the formless skein. She thought of the possibilities, the sheer wonder of what she was doing, the profound implications of this newfound ability.

She finished the scarf quickly, tying off the last knot with a small pair of scissors, the snip echoing loudly in the quiet room. It was a perfectly ordinary scarf, soft and warm, a rich emerald green, about five feet long. Mia held it up, admiring her handiwork, a sense of anticipation bubbling within her.

"Okay, magic scarf, do your thing," she whispered, half-joking, but with a hopeful, almost desperate glint in her eye. She closed her eyes for a moment, picturing a shimmering, flowing silk.

And then, it shimmered.

The emerald green fabric rippled, not like light on water, but as if its very fibers were shifting, rearranging themselves on a molecular level, dissolving and reforming with impossible speed. The soft, woolly texture seemed to smooth, to become impossibly fine, almost translucent, and the color deepened, taking on the lustrous, almost liquid sheen of raw silk, catching the sunlight and refracting it into a thousand tiny rainbows. Mia gasped, her breath catching in her throat. She ran her fingers over it; it felt cool and smooth, exactly like silk, impossibly luxurious. The transformation was complete, seamless, and utterly breathtaking. It was no illusion; the very fabric had changed.

Ethan, having just walked into the room with his coffee mug, stopped dead in his tracks, the aroma of freshly brewed coffee momentarily forgotten. "Whoa," he said, his voice hushed with awe, his eyes wide. "What did you do to that scarf?"

"Watch this," Mia said, her voice barely a whisper, filled with a giddy mixture of triumph and disbelief. She focused again, picturing rough, coarse burlap. The scarf shimmered once more, the silk-like sheen vanishing as if it had never been there, replaced by the dull, earthy tone and nubby, uneven texture of burlap. She rubbed it between her fingers; it felt exactly like burlap, rough and unyielding, surprisingly stiff.

"It can change!" she exclaimed, a joyous, almost hysterical laugh bubbling up inside her. "It can look like anything! Feel like anything!"

Ethan dropped his coffee mug onto the nearest end table with a clatter, spilling a few drops of coffee onto the polished wood. He strode over, snatched the scarf from Mia's hands, and examined it with the intensity of a scientist presented with a new, impossible phenomenon. He felt the burlap, tugged at it, then watched, mesmerized, as Mia, with another surge of concentration, transformed it into a shimmering, almost translucent lace, delicate and intricate, as if spun by a spider. He felt the lace, tracing its delicate patterns, then watched as it became a thick, luxurious velvet, deep and plush, absorbing the light.

"This is… incredible, Mia," he breathed, his skepticism finally, completely, dissolving into pure, unadulterated awe. His logical mind, usually so rigid, was now stretching, bending, trying to encompass this new, impossible reality. "This is real magic."

Over the next few days, Mia experimented relentlessly, her studio becoming a laboratory of enchantment, a vibrant hub of creation. She knitted a small, intricate butterfly, its wings a delicate lacework of yarn in shades of iridescent blue and gold. The moment she finished, it fluttered off her finger, its knitted wings beating silently, gracefully, around the room, casting tiny, dancing shadows on the walls. It landed on a sunbeam, its little body pulsing with a faint, inner light, its antennae twitching with apparent curiosity.

She made a tiny mouse, its whiskers of thread twitching, its button eyes bright with intelligence and mischief. It scurried across the floor with surprising speed, darting under furniture, exploring every nook and cranny, occasionally pausing to sniff at a dust bunny with a discerning air.

Each creation, no matter how small or simple, came to life with a distinct personality. A knitted flower bloomed on her windowsill, its petals unfurling in slow motion, releasing a faint, sweet scent that wasn't quite real, but undeniably there. A tiny knitted bird, no bigger than her thumb, perched on her shoulder and sang a faint, melodious tune, a series of delicate, bell-like notes that filled the room with an ethereal beauty. The house, once filled with the quiet hum of unpacking and the occasional sigh of resignation, was now alive with the gentle rustle of animated yarn, the soft clicks of tiny knitted feet, and the occasional surprised yip from Bean as a knitted creature darted past her nose, or a low, amused rumble from Bear as he watched a knitted squirrel attempt to climb his leg.

And the clothes she made… they were truly extraordinary. A simple knitted dress could transform into a flowing gown of shimmering satin, then a sleek, modern jumpsuit, then a rustic peasant dress, then a military uniform complete with intricate insignia, then a shimmering, almost invisible cloak that seemed to melt into the background, making her virtually undetectable. The possibilities were endless, limited only by her imagination and the amount of yarn she had. The disguises she could create were perfect, seamless, utterly convincing, down to the smallest detail of texture and drape.

The subtle hum of the needles became a comforting presence, a constant reminder of the extraordinary power she now wielded. It was a power that felt ancient, yet intimately connected to her, to her passion for knitting, to the quiet comfort and purpose it had always brought her. She felt a profound connection to her grandmother, as if the magic had been waiting for her, passed down through generations, finally awakening in her hands, a legacy she was only just beginning to understand. She wondered if her grandmother had known, if she had felt the subtle hum, if her own creations had ever briefly flickered with life.

Ethan, for his part, became Mia's most enthusiastic supporter and cautious observer. He'd spend his evenings after work watching her knit, offering suggestions, marveling at each new creation. He even started sketching ideas for knitted gadgets — a grappling hook that could extend indefinitely, a self-tying rope that could knot itself, a blanket that could instantly become a tent, a tiny drone that could scout ahead. His engineering mind, accustomed to the rigid laws of physics, was now playfully grappling with the boundless, illogical possibilities of magic. He found himself sketching complex schematics for how a knitted object might sustain its life, or how the fabric transformations might work on a sub-atomic level, even as he knew such explanations were futile.

"You know," he said one evening, watching a knitted squirrel scamper up the wall and then disappear into a vent, "this is way cooler than anything I do at the plant. My biggest accomplishment today was fixing a leaky valve that was threatening to flood the entire assembly line."

Mia laughed, a genuine, joyful sound that had been rare since their move, a sound that filled the house with warmth. "Well, your leaky valve fixes are probably saving someone a lot of trouble. My squirrel is just… being a squirrel. Albeit, a very adventurous one."

"A *living* squirrel," Ethan corrected, grinning, his eyes twinkling. "Don't forget the 'living' part. That's kind of important. And the fact that it just went into our HVAC system. We might have a knitted rodent problem soon."

But as the days turned into weeks, and Mia continued to explore her newfound abilities, the strange occurrences began to manifest beyond the confines of their little house, spreading like a subtle, magical contagion throughout Newark. Small, inexplicable things at first, easily dismissed by the rational mind, but growing in frequency and intensity. A patch of wildflowers in their backyard, usually a riot of color, suddenly glowed with an ethereal, pulsing light at dusk, casting long, dancing shadows that seemed to move with a life of their own. The old oak tree down the street, a venerable sentinel of the neighborhood, seemed to grow new, unusually vibrant leaves overnight, their emerald green almost too bright, too perfect, shimmering with a faint, internal luminescence.

Whispers started circulating among the locals — hushed tales of odd lights in the sky, not stars or planes, but swirling, colorful auroras that danced briefly before fading. There were reports of strange, melodious sounds carried on the wind that sounded like distant chimes or ethereal singing, too beautiful and otherworldly to be human. Animals, too, began to behave unusually. Birds sang songs never heard before, deer seemed to move with an unnatural grace, and even the local stray cats seemed to possess an uncanny awareness, their eyes glowing faintly in the dark.

Mrs. Gable, their elderly neighbor, a woman known for her meticulously manicured lawn and her even more meticulously cultivated gossip, stopped Mia one morning while she was walking Bean. Mrs. Gable was usually a fount of neighborhood news, but today her eyes were wide with something akin to fear. "Mia, dear," she said, her voice a conspiratorial whisper, her usual briskness replaced by a nervous flutter, "have you noticed anything… peculiar lately?"

Mia feigned innocence, though her heart hammered against her ribs. "Peculiar, Mrs. Gable?"

"Yes! My rose bushes! They've bloomed out of season, in the middle of November, and the petals… they shimmer! Like they're dusted with fairy dust! And just last night, I swear I heard singing from the woods behind the church. Not human singing, mind you. Something… else. Something… ancient." She shivered dramatically, despite the warm morning sun, wrapping her arms around herself. "And my cat, Mittens, she's been staring at the air, batting at nothing, like she sees things we don't."

Mia offered a noncommittal hum, trying to keep her expression neutral, but her mind raced. Fairy dust. Singing. Animals seeing unseen things. It was happening. The magic wasn't confined to her needles anymore. It was seeping into their world, blurring the lines between the mundane and the fantastical, creating a tapestry of strange occurrences that only she and Ethan seemed to fully comprehend.

"Did you hear about Mrs. Henderson's prize-winning pumpkin?" Ethan asked one evening, scrolling through his phone, his brow furrowed in a mixture of amusement and genuine perplexity. "She swears it grew to twice its size overnight, and it's glowing. Like, actually glowing, not just reflecting light." He showed Mia a blurry photo on his phone — a giant, orange orb emitting a soft, golden light from within.

Mia paused, her knitting needles, which had been clicking rhythmically, falling silent. "Glowing?"

"Yeah, like, actually glowing. She thinks it's some kind of new, super-potent fertilizer, but everyone else thinks it's… well, they don't know what they think." He chuckled, but there was a hint of genuine unease in his voice, a subtle shift from playful wonder to something more serious, more ominous. "The local news even did a segment on it. They brought in scientists, botanists, everything. They couldn't explain it. They just called it an 'unprecedented botanical anomaly.'"

Mia had a feeling. A growing, unsettling feeling that these strange occurrences weren't isolated incidents, not random anomalies. They felt connected, somehow, to the magic that now pulsed through her needles, a ripple effect from her own awakening power. It was as if the veil between their world and another was thinning, becoming porous, allowing something extraordinary, something undeniably magical, to seep through. The world, which had once felt so solid and predictable, was now shimmering at the edges, revealing glimpses of something wondrous and terrifying, a hidden reality bleeding into their own.

One Saturday, Mia decided to brave the local farmer's market. She needed fresh produce, and perhaps a distraction from the growing sense of unease that had settled over Newark, a quiet hum of strangeness that permeated the very air. The market was a bustling hub of activity, a kaleidoscope of sights, sounds, and smells. The aroma of freshly baked bread mingled with the sweet scent of ripe berries and the earthy fragrance of freshly dug vegetables. Vendors called out their wares, children laughed, and the murmur of conversation created a comforting background hum. The vibrant chaos was a welcome change from the quiet, unsettling strangeness of their neighborhood.

As she browsed a stall of homemade jams, her gaze fell upon an old woman. She was unlike anyone Mia had ever seen, even in the diverse crowds of Boerne. Her eyes were like polished river stones, ancient and deep, holding a knowing glint that seemed to see right through Mia, straight into her soul. A cascade of silver hair, braided with delicate, shimmering threads that caught the light, fell past her waist, almost touching the ground. She was selling intricate, hand-woven baskets, each one a work of art, woven with patterns that seemed to shift and swirl before Mia's eyes, almost as if they were alive. Some of the baskets even seemed to emit a faint, internal glow.

The woman looked up as Mia approached, a faint, enigmatic smile playing on her lips, a smile that seemed to hold centuries of secrets. "Lovely day for a market, isn't it, dearie?" the old woman rasped, her voice surprisingly strong, yet with an underlying resonance that sent a shiver down Mia's spine, a feeling of profound recognition.

"It is," Mia replied, admiring a particularly beautiful basket woven with what looked like tiny, glowing fibers, almost like spun starlight.

"You have hands that know how to weave," the woman said, her gaze fixed intently on Mia's fingers, which still bore the faint indentations from her knitting needles. "Hands that know the language of thread. Hands that mend."

Mia felt a jolt, a sudden, electric current running through her, a feeling of being exposed, yet strangely understood. "I knit," she corrected, a little defensively, surprised by the woman's directness, by her uncanny perception.

The woman merely smiled, a slow, enigmatic curve of her lips, her eyes twinkling with ancient amusement. "Weaving, knitting, crocheting… all the same, in the grand tapestry. All threads of creation. You feel it, don't you? The thinning of the veil." Her voice was soft, yet it carried an undeniable weight, as if she were speaking of profound, universal truths.

Mia's heart skipped a beat, a frantic drumbeat against her ribs. "The… thinning veil?" she whispered, the words barely audible, her voice trembling.

"Aye," the woman nodded, her gaze drifting to the distant horizon, where the sky seemed to shimmer with an unusual intensity, a faint, almost imperceptible distortion in the air. "The world is restless. A queen in a tower, a shadow of scales, a land in peril. It needs a Weaver of Light. Someone to mend what's broken, to reweave the torn threads of reality." Her eyes, ancient and knowing, met Mia's, and Mia felt an undeniable connection, a sense of being seen, truly seen, for the first time in her life. It was as if the woman was speaking directly to her soul.

Mia stared at her, a chill running down her spine, despite the warmth of the sun. "What are you talking about?" The words tumbled out, a desperate plea for understanding, for a rational explanation.

The old woman leaned closer, her voice dropping to a conspiratorial whisper, yet still carrying that resonant quality, that ancient echo. "Solara. A land of magic, now shrouded in gloom, its vibrant colors muted, its melodies silenced. Its benevolent ruler, Queen Sasha, imprisoned by a mighty dragon, Dreadwing, who serves a dark sorcerer. The balance is broken, child. The threads are frayed, unraveling, and the darkness spreads, even to your world." Her words painted a vivid, terrifying picture in Mia's mind, a world of fantasy suddenly made real, tangible, and dangerously close.

Mia felt an inexplicable pull towards these tales, a strange, profound sense of recognition, as if the old woman was speaking of something she already knew, deep in her bones, a forgotten memory stirring. It was a feeling of destiny, of a path laid out before her, even if she couldn't yet see it clearly, a path she was inexplicably drawn to. "How do you know this?" she asked, her voice trembling with a mixture of fear and fascination, a desperate need for answers.

The woman simply tapped her temple, a faint, knowing smile playing on her lips. "Some things are known, not learned. Some truths are woven into the very fabric of existence. The land cries out. And you, with your hands that weave light, you are meant to hear it. You are meant to answer." She pressed a small, intricately carved wooden charm into Mia's hand. It was smooth and cool, yet radiated a faint warmth, carved with what looked like a stylized tree, its branches intertwined with what could be threads, or perhaps roots, connecting to something ancient and powerful, something alive. "When the time is right, the path will reveal itself. Follow the threads, Weaver. They will guide you."

Before Mia could ask another question, before she could even process the full weight of the woman's words, before she could ask her name or where she came from, the old woman turned, her silver hair shimmering in the sunlight like spun moonlight, and melted into the bustling crowd, as if she were never there at all. One moment she was there, a vibrant, ancient presence; the next, she was gone, leaving only the scent of herbs and a faint, sweet melody lingering in the air. Mia stood there, the wooden charm warm in her palm, her mind reeling, a whirlwind of impossible thoughts and fantastical images. Solara. Queen Sasha. A dragon. A dark sorcerer. It sounded like something out of a fairy tale, yet the old woman's words had resonated with an unsettling truth, a truth that Mia felt deep in her soul, a truth that was now undeniably real.

She hurried home, her head spinning, the charm clutched tightly in her hand, its warmth a constant reminder of the impossible encounter. She found Ethan in the living room, attempting to assemble a notoriously difficult flat-pack bookshelf, a task that usually brought him to the brink of frustration.

Today, he looked unusually calm, almost pensive, as if he too felt the subtle shift in the world.

"Ethan," she began, her voice urgent, her breath still catching in her throat, "you are not going to believe what happened at the market. I met an old woman, and she knew everything." She recounted the old woman's words, the tales of Solara, Queen Sasha, and the dragon Dreadwing, her voice rising with each impossible detail, the story tumbling out in a rush. She described the woman's ancient eyes, her shimmering silver hair, the way she had seemed to vanish into thin air, leaving only the wooden charm.

Ethan, usually so grounded, so logical, listened intently, his screwdriver forgotten in his hand, his gaze fixed on Mia's face, searching for any sign of delusion or fever. When she finished, he was silent for a long moment, the only sound the distant hum of the refrigerator and the gentle rustle of Hopsy attempting to climb the curtains. "A queen in a tower? A dragon? Mia, are you sure you didn't just meet a very imaginative storyteller? Or maybe you were just... tired? Overwhelmed by the move?" He tried to inject a note of reason into his voice, but even he could hear the waver of uncertainty, the tremor of doubt that betrayed his own growing belief.

"It wasn't like that," Mia insisted, her voice firm, unwavering, filled with a conviction that surprised even herself. "She knew about my hands. She knew about… the thinning veil. And the way she spoke, it felt real. Like she was telling me something important, something I needed to hear, something that was meant for me." She held out the wooden charm, its carved surface warm against her palm, a tangible piece of the impossible. "She gave me this. It feels… alive."

Ethan took the charm, turning it over in his fingers. It was smooth, cool, and intricately carved. He traced the stylized tree, its branches intertwined with what could be threads, or perhaps roots, connecting to something ancient and powerful, something that hummed faintly beneath his own touch. "It's beautiful," he admitted, his voice hushed, his skepticism finally giving way to a profound sense of wonder. "But…"

"And the glowing pumpkin," Mia interrupted, her voice gaining momentum, building to a crescendo of revelation. "And the weird lights. And Mrs. Gable's shimmering roses. And the singing in the woods. It's all connected, Ethan. I feel it. This magic, it's not just for making cute animals or changing the texture of a scarf. It's… bigger. It's affecting the world around us. It's bleeding through." She looked at her rosewood needles, lying innocently on the coffee table, catching the light. They seemed to pulse faintly, almost imperceptibly, with a quiet, inner glow, as if responding to her words, to the truth she was speaking aloud.

Ethan looked from the charm to Mia, then to the needles. He was a man of logic, of science, of tangible facts. But he had seen the knitted rabbit hop. He had seen the scarf change its texture and color, effortlessly transforming from silk to burlap to lace to velvet. He couldn't deny what his own eyes had witnessed, what his own hands had touched. The world, as he knew it, was shifting beneath his feet, revealing layers he never knew existed. The impossible was becoming undeniable.

"So," he said slowly, his voice a mixture of awe and disbelief, a hesitant acceptance of the fantastical, "you think… you think there's a real place called Solara, and a real queen named Sasha, and a real dragon named Dreadwing, and that this old woman… she was telling you the absolute, literal truth?"

"I don't know what to think," Mia admitted, running a hand through her hair, a gesture of exasperation and confusion, but also a burgeoning excitement.

"But what if? What if this magic, what if *my* magic, is for a reason? What if I'm supposed to help? What if all these strange things happening in Newark are just… echoes? Ripples from Solara, a cry for help reaching across realms?" The idea, once terrifying, now felt strangely compelling, a call to action she couldn't ignore.

Ethan walked over to her, pulling her into a comforting hug, a solid anchor in the swirling chaos of the unknown. He knew her, knew her kind heart, her unwavering sense of right and wrong, her deep empathy. He knew that when Mia felt a pull, it was usually for a good reason, a moral imperative she couldn't deny. And despite the sheer, mind-boggling impossibility of it all, a part of him, the part that still believed in fairy tales, the part that loved adventure, was thrilled.

"Okay," he said, his voice firm, his resolve hardening, a quiet strength emanating from him. "Okay. Let's find out. Let's research this Solara. Let's see if there's anything, anything at all, that points to this being real. We'll go to the library, we'll look online, we'll talk to anyone who might know anything. We'll exhaust every possibility before we dismiss it." He pulled back slightly, looking into her eyes. "If this is real, if you're meant to help, then we'll do it. Together."

Chapter 3: Echoes from Another Realm

The wooden charm, warm and smooth in Mia's palm, felt like a tangible piece of the impossible, a silent promise whispered across realms. Its intricate carving, a stylized tree with intertwined branches that seemed to pulse with a faint, internal light, was a constant reminder of the old woman's words: *Solara. Queen Sasha. A mighty dragon. A Weaver of Light.* The fantastical narrative, once confined to the realm of children's stories, had abruptly crashed into their quiet, suburban reality, ushered in by the impossible magic of Mia's knitting needles.

Ethan, ever the pragmatist, was already pulling out his laptop, his fingers flying across the keyboard with a renewed sense of purpose. "Okay, 'Solara'," he muttered, typing the name into a search engine. "Let's see what the internet has to say about a magical land with a dragon problem."

Mia watched him, a knot of apprehension and excitement tightening in her stomach. "You really think we'll find anything?"

"At this point, Mia, I'm not ruling anything out," he replied, his eyes glued to the screen. "We have a living knitted rabbit, a scarf that changes its molecular structure, and a neighbor who swears her pumpkin is glowing. A hidden magical realm doesn't seem that far-fetched anymore." He flashed her a quick, reassuring smile, but his brow was furrowed in concentration.

Their initial searches were, predictably, fruitless. "Solara" yielded results about ancient Anglo-Saxon kingdoms, historical figures, and obscure literary references, but nothing resembling a current, magical land. "Queen Sasha" brought up pop stars and historical monarchs, none of whom were imprisoned by dragons. "Dreadwing" was a brand of industrial lubricant.

"Well, that was anticlimactic," Ethan sighed after an hour, leaning back in his chair, running a hand through his already disheveled hair. "Looks like Google isn't quite up to speed on interdimensional travel."

Mia didn't feel defeated. A strange sense of calm had settled over her, a quiet certainty that the old woman hadn't been lying. "Maybe it's not something you can just Google," she suggested, picking up her rosewood needles, their familiar weight a comfort in her hand. The subtle hum was still there, a constant, gentle vibration that seemed to whisper secrets only she could hear. "Maybe it's hidden. Or forgotten."

"Hidden and forgotten is my specialty," Ethan declared, pushing himself up. "Alright, Plan B. Libraries. Old books. Obscure folklore. Anything that predates the internet."

The next few days became a blur of research. Ethan, with his methodical engineering mind, approached it like a complex problem to be solved. He mapped out local libraries, cross-referenced historical societies, and even delved into academic databases for obscure anthropological texts. Mia, guided by her intuition and the subtle pull she felt towards anything that resonated with the old woman's words, focused on local legends, forgotten myths, and anything that hinted at a "thinning veil" or hidden pathways.

They spent hours at the Newark Public Library, a charming, albeit small, building with a surprisingly robust local history section. The air was thick with the scent of old paper and dust, a comforting aroma to Mia, who loved the tangible feel of a book in her hands. They unearthed dusty tomes on Arkansas folklore, collections of Ozark mountain legends, and even a few self-published pamphlets on local ghost stories and unexplained phenomena.

"Listen to this," Ethan said one afternoon, his voice hushed, reading from a brittle, yellowed book titled

"Whispers of the Ozarks." "'It is said that in the deepest hollows, where the ancient trees stand sentinel, the veil between worlds grows thin. On nights of the twin moons, or when the stars align in a forgotten pattern, one might glimpse the shimmer of another realm, or hear the distant song of its inhabitants.'" He looked at Mia, his eyes wide. "Twin moons? Distant song? That sounds a lot like what Mrs. Gable was talking about."

Mia nodded, her own heart quickening. "And the shimmering roses. And the glowing pumpkin. It's not just our house, Ethan. It's the whole town. The veil *is* thinning."

The strange occurrences in Newark continued to escalate, no longer just whispers but undeniable phenomena. The glowing pumpkin, Mrs. Henderson's pride and joy, became a local sensation, drawing curious onlookers and even a few bewildered scientists from the nearest university. Its soft, golden luminescence pulsed gently, illuminating Mrs. Henderson's porch like a mystical beacon. The rose bushes in Mrs. Gable's yard, once merely vibrant, now shimmered with an almost liquid light, their petals unfurling in impossible, intricate patterns.

The "singing from the woods" became more distinct. It wasn't just chimes anymore; it was a complex, ethereal melody, sometimes sounding like a chorus of unseen voices, sometimes like the mournful cry of an unknown creature. It resonated deep within Mia, a haunting beauty that stirred something ancient in her soul. Bean and Bear, too, reacted to it. Bean would cock her head, whimpering softly, while Bear would stand at the back door, his hackles slightly raised, a low growl rumbling in his chest, as if sensing something both beautiful and dangerous.

One evening, while walking the dogs, Mia saw it. A faint, shimmering distortion in the air above the old, abandoned mill on the outskirts of town. It was like heat haze, but it pulsed with faint, iridescent colors — greens, blues, purples — shifting and swirling like oil on water. It lasted only a moment, then vanished, leaving the air still and ordinary. But Mia knew what she had seen. The veil.

Ethan, despite his scientific background, found himself increasingly unable to offer rational explanations. He'd tried to measure the energy output of the glowing pumpkin, but his instruments malfunctioned. He'd recorded the strange singing, but the audio files were filled with static and unidentifiable frequencies. He was forced to confront the undeniable truth: magic was real, and it was actively manifesting in their world.

"It's like… a bleed-through," he mused one night, sketching furiously in a notebook, trying to diagram the inexplicable. "Whatever's happening in Solara, it's affecting our reality. Like two membranes pressing against each other, and the pressure is causing tears."

Mia looked at her needles. "And my needles are… a part of it. A conduit. Maybe they're not just creating magic, but reacting to it. Amplifying it."

The idea settled between them, a heavy, yet exhilarating truth. Mia's magic wasn't an isolated phenomenon; it was intrinsically linked to the larger magical disturbance affecting Newark. This meant her gift wasn't just a whimsical talent; it was a tool, perhaps even a weapon, in a conflict she was only just beginning to understand.

Their research eventually led them to the dusty archives of the county historical society, a place few people ever visited. It was a treasure trove of forgotten documents, old maps, and faded photographs. After days of sifting through mundane records, Ethan let out a triumphant shout.

"Mia! Get over here! You are not going to believe this!"

He was hunched over a large, leather-bound journal, its pages brittle with age. It was a personal diary, meticulously kept by a woman named Elara Vance, who had lived in Newark in the late 1800s. Her elegant, looping script filled the pages, detailing daily life, local events, and, increasingly, strange occurrences.

"Listen to this entry, from October 1897," Ethan read, his voice trembling slightly with excitement. "'The air grows heavy with unseen energies. The woods whisper of ancient powers, and the very stars seem to shift in their courses. My grandmother spoke of such times, when the veil thinned, and echoes of Solara bled into our world. She spoke of a queen, imprisoned by a great beast, and a sorcerer who sought to unravel the threads of creation itself. And of a Weaver, whose hands held the power to mend what was broken, to reweave the tapestry of reality.'"

Mia gasped, her hand flying to her mouth. "Solara! A Weaver! It's all here!"

Ethan continued, his voice barely above a whisper. "'My grandmother believed the gateway lay hidden in the old, forgotten grove, where the ancient standing stones hummed with a quiet power. She said only those with a pure heart and a weaver's touch could perceive it, could step through the shimmering threshold.'"

The journal detailed Elara Vance's own attempts to find the gateway, her growing despair as the magical echoes faded, and her eventual conclusion that the time was not yet right for the Weaver to emerge. She had meticulously drawn a crude map in the back of the journal, marking the location of the "forgotten grove" just outside of Newark, a place Mia knew well from their dog walks.

"The forgotten grove," Mia breathed, her mind racing. She remembered the old, gnarled trees, the strangely smooth, moss-covered stones that seemed to be arranged in a deliberate pattern, a place that had always felt oddly serene, almost sacred. She had dismissed it as a natural formation, but now…

"This is it, Mia," Ethan said, closing the journal gently, as if afraid to disturb its ancient secrets. "This is our answer. Solara is real. Queen Sasha is real. The dragon, Dreadwing, is real. And you… you are the Weaver."

The weight of the revelation settled heavily on Mia. It wasn't just a fun, magical hobby anymore. It was a calling. A destiny. And it was terrifying. She was Mia

Martinez, a graphic designer from Boerne, Texas, who liked to knit. She wasn't a hero. She wasn't a warrior. How could she possibly face a dragon and a dark sorcerer?

Ethan seemed to read her thoughts. He reached across the table, taking her hand. "Hey. We're in this together. You're not alone. And you have magic knitting needles, which, let's be honest, is a pretty good superpower." He squeezed her hand. "We'll figure it out. One stitch at a time."

His unwavering support was a lifeline. Ethan, with his grounded nature and practical mind, was the perfect counterpoint to Mia's newfound, overwhelming magical reality. He didn't question *if* she could do it, only *how*.

They spent the rest of the day planning. If the gateway was in the forgotten grove, they needed to be prepared. Mia considered what she might need to knit for such a journey. Disguises, definitely. A shimmering cloak that could turn invisible, or blend into any environment. Perhaps a sturdy rope, or a net. Animated creatures for distraction, or even for carrying messages. The possibilities were endless, but she needed to be strategic. She couldn't just knit random things; each creation had to serve a purpose.

Ethan, meanwhile, focused on the practicalities. Food, water, first-aid supplies, a flashlight, a compass (though he suspected it might go haywire in a magical realm). He even packed a small, portable charging bank for their phones, just in case. "You never know," he said with a wry grin, "maybe Solara has Wi-Fi."

Bean and Bear, sensing the shift in their humans' energy, were unusually attentive. Bean would nudge Mia's hand, as if offering comfort, while Bear would lie at their feet, his large head resting on his paws, his eyes following their every move, a silent, watchful presence. They seemed to understand the gravity of the situation, their animal instincts attuned to the subtle shifts in the magical currents that now permeated their home.

Mia looked at the old, faded map in Elara Vance's journal. The "forgotten grove" was a short hike from their house, a place they had walked the dogs countless times. It was unsettling to think that a portal to another world had been right under their noses all along.

The night before they planned to venture into the grove, Mia couldn't sleep. She lay awake, listening to the strange, ethereal singing from the woods, now louder, more insistent. It felt like a siren song, calling her, beckoning her to step through the veil. She thought of Queen Sasha, imprisoned and suffering. She thought of a land shrouded in gloom, waiting for a Weaver of Light.

Fear was a cold knot in her stomach, but beneath it, a spark of determination glowed. She was Mia Martinez, from Boerne, Texas. She might not be a hero, but she had a gift. And if that gift could help someone, could save a land, then she had to try. She wouldn't be doing it alone. She had Ethan, her logical, supportive anchor. And she had Hopsy, and her other knitted creations, tiny miracles that proved the impossible was real.

As dawn broke, painting the sky in hues of soft pink and gold, Mia rose. She carefully packed her rosewood needles, a generous supply of yarn in various colors and textures, and the wooden charm. She looked at Ethan, still asleep, his face peaceful. She knew this journey would change them forever.

The air outside was crisp, carrying the scent of damp earth and the faint, sweet perfume of Mrs. Gable's shimmering roses. The glowing pumpkin on Mrs. Henderson's porch pulsed softly in the pre-dawn light, a silent beacon. Bean and Bear, sensing the impending adventure, were already at the door, tails wagging, their eyes bright with anticipation.

Mia took a deep breath. The veil was thinning. The threads were calling. And she, the Weaver of Light, was ready to follow them. The threshold awaited.

Chapter 4: The Quest Unravels

The revelation from Elara Vance's journal hung in the air between Mia and Ethan, a pronouncement of destiny that was both exhilarating and terrifying. *Solara is real. Queen Sasha is real. The dragon, Dreadwing, is real. And you… you are the Weaver.* The words echoed in Mia's mind, each syllable a hammer blow against the comfortable walls of her ordinary life. She was Mia Martinez, a graphic designer from Boerne, Texas, who liked to knit cozy sweaters and whimsical toys. She wasn't a hero. She wasn't a warrior. The idea of facing a dragon, let alone a dark sorcerer, felt utterly absurd, a plot point ripped from a fantasy novel, not a chapter in her own life.

Fear, cold and sharp, coiled in her stomach. How could she, a woman whose greatest challenge until recently had been untangling a particularly stubborn knot of yarn, possibly mend the fabric of reality? What did a "Weaver of Light" even do in a confrontation with a "Shadow of Scales"? Her magic, while undeniably real and wondrous, felt small, domestic. Animated knitted animals and transforming scarves seemed ill-equipped for a battle against ancient evil.

Ethan, sensing her spiraling thoughts, reached across the table, his hand warm and solid over hers. "Hey," he said, his voice gentle but firm. "We're in this together. You're not alone. And you have magic knitting needles, which, let's be honest, is a pretty good superpower." He squeezed her hand, his gaze unwavering. "We'll figure it out. One stitch at a time."

His unwavering support was a lifeline, an anchor in the swirling chaos of her mind. Ethan, with his grounded nature and practical mind, was the perfect counterpoint to Mia's newfound, overwhelming magical reality. He didn't question *if* she could do it, only *how*. His belief in her, even in the face of the utterly impossible, was a powerful force.

They spent the rest of the day planning, the journal spread open between them, its crude map of the "forgotten grove" now a blueprint for their impossible journey. If the gateway was indeed hidden there, they needed to be prepared. This wasn't a casual stroll in the park; it was an expedition into the unknown, a potential confrontation with forces beyond their comprehension.

Mia's first thought turned to her knitting. Her magic was her only weapon, her only tool. She needed to be strategic, to think not just of what she *could* knit, but what she *needed* to knit. The whimsical creations of the past few weeks – Hopsy, the butterfly, the tiny mouse – were delightful, but they wouldn't save a queen from a dragon.

"Disguises," she murmured, tracing a finger over the map. "We'll need disguises. Something that can blend in, or make us invisible." She pulled out a skein of dark, almost black yarn, its fibers surprisingly strong. "A shimmering cloak. Something that can turn invisible, or blend into any environment." She envisioned a cloak that could mimic stone, shadow, even the very air, making them ghosts in the castle corridors. The rosewood needles hummed in anticipation as she began to cast on, the first stitches imbued with a fierce determination.

As she knitted, the magic flowed, stronger and more responsive than ever before. The cloak grew rapidly, its fabric shifting subtly even as she worked, hinting at its chameleon-like properties. She focused on the intention: *concealment, invisibility, seamless blending.* The yarn seemed to melt and reform under her fingers, the stitches tightening and loosening with an intelligence of their own.

"What else?" Ethan prompted, watching her hands move with a mesmerized fascination. "Think practical. What would an engineer need in a fantasy land?"

"A rope," Mia decided, her needles already clicking with a new rhythm. "A sturdy, unbreakable rope. One that can extend indefinitely, or tie itself." She chose a thick, natural-colored hemp yarn, focusing on *strength, flexibility, infinite length*. As she knitted, the rope grew surprisingly quickly, coiling on the floor like a living snake, its texture rough and strong, yet soft to the touch. She tugged at it, and it seemed to stretch, then retract, confirming its magical elasticity.

"And maybe… a net?" Ethan suggested, his mind already running through scenarios. "For capturing, or for climbing."

Mia nodded, switching to a finer, almost invisible yarn. "A net. Light, strong, and maybe… self-repairing." She pictured a net that could mend itself if torn, a web of magic that would hold firm against any strain. The intricate lacework of the net began to form, impossibly delicate yet radiating an undeniable strength.

Then came the animated creatures. "We'll need distractions," Mia mused. "Lots of them. And maybe… scouts. Messengers." She decided on a flock of knitted birds, small and swift, that could fly ahead, observe, and return with information. She chose bright, vibrant yarns for contrast, so they could easily spot them. As she knitted each bird, she focused on *speed, agility, keen sight*. The moment she finished the last stitch, each bird fluttered to life, chirping softly, their tiny knitted eyes bright with intelligence. They perched on her shoulder, on Ethan's head, on the back of the armchair, a silent, colorful army in miniature. She also knitted a few more Hopsy-like rabbits, larger this time, with a focus on *speed and diversion*, envisioning them creating chaos in the castle.

Ethan, meanwhile, focused on the mundane, yet equally crucial, practicalities. He meticulously checked their existing camping gear. Food that wouldn't spoil easily: energy bars, dried fruit, jerky. Water bottles, a portable filter, just in case. A comprehensive first-aid kit, stocked with bandages, antiseptic, pain relievers. A high-powered flashlight, extra batteries. A sturdy compass, though he suspected it might go haywire in a magical realm. He even packed a small, portable charging bank for their phones. "You never know," he said with a wry grin, tucking it into his backpack, "maybe Solara has Wi-Fi, or at least a magical outlet."

They discussed the risks, the sheer unknown they were stepping into. "We don't know what kind of magic the sorcerer has," Ethan cautioned. "Or how powerful Dreadwing is. We need to be careful, Mia. This isn't a game."

"I know," she replied, her voice soft, but firm. "But we can't just ignore it, can we? Not after everything. Not after finding Elara Vance's journal. Not when Newark is… changing."

The escalating magical bleed-through in Newark made their departure feel less like a choice and more like an urgent necessity. The strange phenomena became more frequent, more pronounced, harder to ignore. The glowing pumpkin on Mrs. Henderson's porch pulsed with a more intense, almost rhythmic beat, casting long, dancing shadows that seemed to writhe with a life of their own. Mrs. Gable's shimmering roses now emitted a faint, sweet perfume that was intoxicating, almost dizzying, and their petals unfurled into impossible, geometric patterns that defied botanical logic.

The "singing from the woods" was no longer distant. It swelled and faded, sometimes sounding like a chorus of unseen voices, sometimes like the mournful cry of an unknown creature, sometimes like a joyous, triumphant anthem. It permeated the very air, a constant, ethereal soundtrack to their increasingly surreal existence. Bean and Bear, too, reacted to it with growing intensity. Bean would cock her head, whimpering softly, her ears twitching, as if trying to pinpoint the source of the sound, while Bear would stand at the back door, his hackles slightly raised, a low growl rumbling in his chest, as if sensing something both beautiful and dangerous, a primal instinct warning him of a world out of balance.

One morning, Mia woke to find a delicate, shimmering frost covering their entire backyard, despite the mild autumn temperatures. It wasn't ice; it was a crystalline substance that sparkled with every color of the rainbow, melting into nothingness the moment the sun touched it. Another evening, the stars in the night sky seemed to shift, briefly forming constellations that Mia had never seen before, patterns that pulsed with an unnatural light before snapping back into their familiar arrangements. The veil was not just thinning; it was tearing.

Mia and Ethan found themselves whispering about these things, afraid to speak too loudly, as if acknowledging them too openly would somehow make them more real, more dangerous. But they were real. The magic was here, in their world, and it was a direct consequence of the turmoil in Solara. Their mission felt increasingly vital, not just for a faraway queen, but for the stability of their own reality.

The night before they planned to venture into the forgotten grove, Mia couldn't sleep. She lay awake, listening to the strange, ethereal singing from the woods, now louder, more insistent, almost a physical presence in the air. It felt like a siren song, calling her, beckoning her to step through the veil, to answer the silent plea of a suffering land. She thought of Queen Sasha, imprisoned and suffering. She thought of a land shrouded in gloom, waiting for a Weaver of Light.

She got out of bed, careful not to wake Ethan, and walked to the window. The moon, a bright, full orb, hung in the sky, but beside it, a faint, ghostly second moon, a shimmering, translucent sphere, was barely visible. The "twin moons" from Elara Vance's journal. A celestial alignment, a sign that the time was indeed right.

Fear was a cold knot in her stomach, a constant companion, but beneath it, a spark of determination glowed, fierce and unyielding. She was Mia Martinez, from Boerne, Texas. She might not be a hero in the traditional sense, but she had a gift. And if that gift could help someone, could save a land, then she had to try. She wouldn't be doing it alone. She had

Ethan, her logical, supportive anchor, her steadfast companion. And she had Hopsy, and her other knitted creations, tiny miracles that proved the impossible was real, that magic existed, and that she was a part of it.

She thought of her grandmother, whose hands had taught her to knit, whose quiet wisdom had always guided her. She felt a connection to a lineage of Weavers, a responsibility she hadn't known she possessed. This wasn't just about rescuing a queen; it was about protecting worlds, about mending the very fabric of existence.

As dawn broke, painting the sky in hues of soft pink and molten gold, Mia rose. She carefully packed her rosewood needles, a generous supply of yarn in various colors and textures, and the wooden charm, now nestled safely in her pocket. She looked at Ethan, still asleep, his face peaceful, unaware of the profound shift in the world outside. She knew this journey would change them forever, irrevocably altering the course of their lives.

The air outside was crisp, carrying the scent of damp earth and the faint, sweet perfume of Mrs. Gable's shimmering roses, now glowing with an almost blinding intensity. The glowing pumpkin on Mrs. Henderson's porch pulsed softly in the pre-dawn light, a silent, mystical beacon guiding their way. Bean and Bear, sensing the impending adventure, were already at the door, tails wagging with an unusual fervor, their eyes bright with anticipation, their animal instincts fully attuned to the magical currents that now permeated their home.

They ate a quick, silent breakfast, the tension thick but not oppressive. It was the quiet before a storm, the calm before a momentous leap. Ethan shouldered his backpack, Mia hers, her knitting bag slung across her body. Hopsy, the knitted rabbit, sat perched on Ethan's shoulder, its button eyes wide and alert. The knitted birds fluttered around Mia's head, then settled on her backpack, ready for their mission.

"Ready?" Ethan asked, his voice steady, his hand reaching for hers.

Mia took a deep breath, the scent of magic and damp earth filling her lungs. "As I'll ever be."

They stepped out of the house, leaving behind the comforting familiarity of their new home, and began their walk towards the forgotten grove. The neighborhood was quiet, still asleep, but the magic was undeniably awake. The leaves on the trees shimmered with unnatural colors, the grass seemed to vibrate with unseen energy, and the air itself felt alive, thick with anticipation.

As they approached the outskirts of town, the mundane gradually gave way to the mystical. The paved roads turned into overgrown dirt paths, the suburban houses faded into the distance, replaced by ancient, gnarled trees whose branches twisted into impossible shapes. The "forgotten grove" was even more pronounced than Mia remembered from their casual dog walks. The trees here were older, taller, their roots snaking across the ground like ancient serpents. The air grew heavier, thick with an almost palpable energy, a sense of immense power contained just beneath the surface.

And then they saw them: the ancient standing stones. They were massive, rough-hewn monoliths, arranged in a rough circle, half-buried in the moss-covered earth. Mia had always dismissed them as natural rock formations, but now, seeing them with new eyes, she realized their deliberate placement, their silent, watchful presence. They hummed with a quiet power, a low, resonant thrum that vibrated through the ground, up through her feet, and into her very bones. The wooden charm in her pocket grew warm, pulsing in sync with the stones.

Bean and Bear, usually eager to chase squirrels in the grove, were subdued. Bean whimpered softly, pressing close to Mia's leg, while Bear circled the stones cautiously, his low growl a constant rumble in his chest, his golden fur bristling. They sensed the immense power, the threshold they were approaching.

They walked to the center of the circle, where the largest stone stood, taller than Ethan, its surface covered in ancient, indecipherable carvings that seemed to shift and swirl in the dappled sunlight. The air around it shimmered with an increasing intensity, the iridescent colors Mia had seen above the mill now swirling around the stone, coalescing into a vibrant, pulsating vortex.

The "shimmering threshold" from Elara Vance's journal.

The vortex grew, expanding from the center of the stone, twisting and turning like a liquid rainbow, pulling at the air around it. It hummed with a deep, resonant sound, a melody that was both alien and strangely familiar, echoing the "singing from the woods" but infinitely more powerful, more profound. It was a gateway, a window into another world, opening before their eyes.

Mia looked at Ethan, her eyes wide with awe and a lingering trace of fear. He squeezed her hand, a silent promise. They both knew there was no turning back. Their world was calling them, but another world was calling louder.

They took a collective breath. Bean, with a soft whimper, nudged Mia's leg, then looked up at her, her eyes filled with trust. Bear, after one last, deep rumble, lowered his hackles and pressed against Ethan, ready.

Mia clutched her rosewood needles, their hum a comforting thrum against her palm. She looked at the shimmering vortex, its colors swirling, beckoning. This was it. The leap of faith. The beginning of their true adventure.

With a shared glance, a silent pact, Mia and Ethan stepped forward, into the shimmering threshold, Bean and Bear following closely behind them. The world around them dissolved into a kaleidoscope of light and sound, a sensation of falling and soaring all at once. The scent of damp earth and roses vanished, replaced by an aroma of strange, sweet blossoms and something metallic, ancient. The sounds of Newark faded, replaced by the ethereal singing and a faint, distant roar that resonated with primal power.

They were no longer in Newark, Arkansas. They were in Solara. And the quest had truly begun.

Chapter 5: Crossing the Threshold

The kaleidoscope of light and sound that engulfed Mia and Ethan as they stepped through the shimmering threshold was an assault on every sense, a disorienting symphony of the impossible. Colors exploded around them – not the familiar hues of their world, but incandescent, pulsating shades of violet, emerald, and gold that swirled and merged like liquid nebulae. Sounds wrapped around them, a cacophony of distant chimes, a low, resonant hum that vibrated in their bones, and a faint, mournful wail that seemed to echo from the very fabric of existence. The sensation was one of falling and soaring simultaneously, a dizzying plunge through an ethereal tunnel that stretched beyond comprehension.

Mia instinctively squeezed Ethan's hand, her knuckles white, her knitting bag clutched tightly to her chest. Her rosewood needles, nestled safely within, hummed with a frantic energy, their warmth spreading through her body like a protective aura. Bean, with a soft whimper, buried her head against Mia's leg, trembling, while Bear, despite his massive size, pressed tightly against Ethan, his usual boisterous energy replaced by a deep, guttural whine of disorientation. The dogs, too, were experiencing the profound shift, their animal instincts overwhelmed by the sheer sensory overload.

Just as the disorientation threatened to consume them, the swirling vortex abruptly dissipated. They landed with a soft thud on what felt like moss, the impact surprisingly gentle. The blinding light receded, replaced by a soft, diffused glow that seemed to emanate from the very air itself.

Mia blinked, her eyes adjusting, and gasped.

They were no longer in the familiar, autumnal woods of Newark, Arkansas. They stood in a clearing of impossible beauty, yet tinged with an undeniable melancholy. The trees that surrounded them were unlike anything Mia had ever seen. Their trunks, gnarled and ancient, twisted upwards like living sculptures, their bark shimmering with faint, opalescent patterns. Their leaves, instead of green, were a vibrant, pulsing sapphire, catching the light and casting an ethereal blue glow on the forest floor. Strange, luminescent flora bloomed at their feet – flowers that glowed with soft, internal lights, their petals unfurling in slow, deliberate movements, and fungi that pulsed with a faint, rhythmic beat.

The air itself was different. It was thick with a sweet, earthy scent, mingled with the metallic tang of something ancient and powerful, and a faint, underlying aroma of decay, like forgotten dreams. The sky above, visible through the canopy of sapphire leaves, was a swirling canvas of deep indigo and violet, pierced by stars that seemed larger, brighter, and arranged in unfamiliar constellations. And there, hanging prominently, was not one moon, but two: a large, radiant orb, casting a silvery glow, and beside it, a smaller, translucent sphere, shimmering with an inner light, just as Elara Vance's journal had described. The twin moons.

Solara.

The name whispered through Mia's mind, a realization that settled deep in her bones, both terrifying and exhilarating. This was it. This was the land from the legends, the place that had bled into their world, the source of the magic that now coursed through her veins.

But despite the breathtaking beauty, an undeniable sense of sadness permeated the air. The vibrant colors seemed muted, the glowing flora pulsed with a faint, almost desperate energy, and the melodic hum that filled the forest was tinged with a mournful undertone. It was a land of magic, yes, but a magic that was suffering, a beauty that was in pain.

Ethan, equally stunned, let out a slow whistle. "Well," he breathed, his voice hushed with awe, "this certainly isn't Arkansas anymore." He reached out, touching a glowing flower, its petals warm and soft beneath his fingertips. "It's… beautiful. But also… sad."

Bean, after her initial shock, began to sniff the glowing moss beneath her paws, her tail giving a tentative wag. Bear, ever the protector, let out a low, inquisitive rumble, his nose twitching as he took in the myriad new scents. Their fear seemed to have given way to a cautious curiosity, their animal instincts adapting with surprising speed to the alien environment.

"We need to move," Mia said, her voice a little shaky, but firm. The realization of where they were, and *why* they were there, spurred her into action. "The castle. We need to find the castle. And Queen Sasha."

They consulted Elara Vance's crude map, which, to their surprise, seemed to resonate with the magical energies of Solara. The lines on the parchment glowed faintly, pointing them towards a distant, ominous mountain range that pierced the violet sky. Atop its highest peak, a dark, jagged silhouette was barely visible – the castle.

Their journey began through the sapphire forest. The ground was soft and springy with moss, making their footsteps almost silent. The air was cool, but not cold, and filled with the gentle hum of unseen life. Strange, ethereal creatures flitted through the trees – tiny, glowing sprites that resembled fireflies, and larger, shadowy forms that darted through the undergrowth, too fast to properly identify.

Mia quickly realized the value of her knitted creations. The knitted birds she'd made, perched on her backpack, chirped softly, their tiny knitted eyes bright and alert. They would occasionally dart ahead, returning moments later with a soft flutter, indicating a clear path or a potential obstacle. They were invaluable scouts, their keen sight and agility perfectly suited for navigating the dense, magical forest.

The shimmering cloak proved equally essential. As they walked, Mia focused on its chameleon-like properties, willing it to mimic the shifting patterns of the sapphire leaves, the dappled light of the forest floor, or the rough texture of the ancient tree trunks. The cloak rippled, its fabric dissolving into its surroundings, making them almost invisible to the casual observer. They moved like ghosts through the forest, unseen, unheard, a silent testament to Mia's growing mastery of her magic.

Ethan, ever the engineer, found himself constantly analyzing the environment. He noted the strange, almost crystalline structure of the glowing flora, the way the light seemed to be absorbed and re-emitted by the very air. He tested the strength of the magical rope Mia had knitted, finding it impossibly strong, capable of supporting both their weights with ease. He used it to swing across a small, glowing chasm, and to pull himself up a steep, moss-covered incline. His practical mind, though still grappling with the *how* of it all, was quickly adapting to the *what if.*

Their first real challenge came late in the afternoon. The sapphire forest gave way to a winding river, its waters not clear, but a swirling vortex of deep indigo and silver, reflecting the twin moons in its depths. The river was wide, its currents swift, and there was no bridge in sight.

"Well, this is a problem," Ethan muttered, peering into the swirling water. "Looks too fast to swim, and too wide to jump."

Mia looked at her magical rope. "The rope can extend indefinitely, right?"

Ethan nodded. "In theory. We haven't tested 'indefinitely' yet."

"Let's try," Mia said, her mind already working. "If we can get it across, we can use it to pull ourselves over."

She focused on the rope, willing it to stretch, to reach the far bank. The hemp yarn seemed to lengthen, uncoiling itself with a soft, almost imperceptible hiss, stretching across the churning indigo water. It reached the other side, wrapping itself around a gnarled, glowing tree trunk.

"Okay, that's step one," Ethan said, impressed. "Now, how do we get across without falling in?"

Mia looked at the net she had knitted, light and strong. "The net. We can use it like a makeshift bridge. And if it tears, it can repair itself."

They worked together, Ethan securing one end of the rope, Mia securing the other. Then, carefully, Mia began to knit the net onto the rope, creating a narrow, flexible pathway across the river. The knitted birds fluttered overhead, chirping encouragement. Hopsy, perched on Ethan's shoulder, twitched its nose, as if offering strategic advice.

It was slow, painstaking work. The magic of the river seemed to resist the net, pulling at the threads, trying to unravel them. Mia had to concentrate fiercely, pouring her will into each stitch, willing the net to hold, to mend itself whenever a thread threatened to snap. Ethan provided steady support, holding the rope taut, his presence a calming anchor.

Finally, after what felt like hours, the net-bridge was complete. It swayed precariously over the indigo river, but it held.

"You first," Ethan said, gesturing to Mia. "You're lighter."

Mia took a deep breath, her heart pounding. She stepped onto the net, testing its strength. It held. Slowly, carefully, she began to cross, her eyes fixed on the far bank. Bean, whimpering softly, followed close behind her, her paws surprisingly nimble on the unstable surface.

Ethan followed, Bear padding carefully behind him, his large frame making the net sag slightly, but it held firm, its self-repairing magic subtly mending any strain. They made it across, breathless but triumphant.

"That was… exhilarating," Ethan said, once they were safely on the other side, the rope and net retracting back into Mia's bag. "Your magic is seriously impressive, Mia."

Mia smiled, a genuine, joyful smile. With every successful use of her magic, her confidence grew, replacing the initial fear with a burgeoning sense of power and purpose. She was learning, adapting, becoming the Weaver of Light.

As they continued their journey, the landscape began to change. The sapphire forest thinned, giving way to rolling hills covered in shimmering, iridescent grasses that swayed in the gentle breeze, resembling a vast, living tapestry. The air here was clearer, but the pervasive sense of melancholy remained, almost stronger, as if the land itself was weeping.

They encountered strange creatures – herds of graceful, multi-limbed deer with antlers that glowed faintly, and shy, furry beings that resembled oversized squirrels, their eyes like polished emeralds. Mia's knitted animals seemed to communicate with them, Hopsy twitching its nose in greeting, the knitted birds chirping in what sounded like a friendly conversation. It was a world teeming with life, but a life that seemed subdued, waiting for something to awaken it.

The sun, or rather, the primary moon, began to set, casting long, violet shadows across the hills. The twin moons rose higher, their combined light illuminating the landscape with an ethereal glow. They decided to make camp for the night.

Ethan found a sheltered hollow, and Mia, with a thought, knitted a small, sturdy tent from a skein of dark, camouflaged yarn. The tent instantly unfolded, its fabric shifting to blend seamlessly with the surrounding environment, making it almost invisible. Inside, it was surprisingly spacious and warm. She then knitted a soft, thick blanket, its fibers imbued with a subtle warmth, providing comfort against the cool night air.

As they settled down, Mia pulled out her needles again. She felt a need to create, to bring more life into this subdued world. She began to knit a collection of small, glowing lanterns, each one a tiny sphere of yarn that emitted a soft, warm light. She hung them around the tent, creating a cozy, magical glow.

"You know," Ethan said, watching her, "it's amazing how quickly you've adapted to all this. One minute you're knitting a rabbit, the next you're building magical bridges and camouflaged tents."

Mia shrugged, a small smile playing on her lips. "It just… feels right. Like I was meant to do this. Like the needles are guiding me." She looked at her rosewood needles, their hum a steady, comforting presence. "It's like they have a will of their own, sometimes. A purpose."

They talked late into the night, discussing their plan, the challenges ahead, and the sheer audacity of their mission. They were just two people from Texas, armed with magic knitting needles and a backpack of supplies, attempting to rescue a queen from a dragon in another dimension. It was insane. But it was also undeniably real.

The next morning, they continued their journey, the castle's silhouette growing steadily larger on the horizon. The landscape became more desolate, the vibrant flora replaced by thorny, skeletal trees and jagged rock formations. The air grew colder, heavier, and the pervasive melancholy deepened into a palpable sense of dread. The silence here was oppressive, broken only by the mournful whispers of the wind.

They knew they were getting closer to the heart of the darkness, to the source of Solara's suffering. The magic of the land, once vibrant and beautiful, now felt twisted, corrupted. The ground beneath their feet seemed to thrum with a dark energy, and the sky above the castle was a perpetual bruise of stormy clouds, pierced by occasional flashes of dark lightning.

Their next significant challenge came as they approached the foothills of the mountain range where the castle resided. The path became treacherous, winding through a narrow gorge lined with sharp, obsidian-like rocks. Suddenly, the ground beneath them trembled, and a low, guttural growl echoed through the gorge, shaking the very air.

A creature emerged from the shadows, blocking their path. It was a monstrosity of jagged rock and twisted roots, its eyes glowing with malevolent red light. It was a Golem, animated by dark magic, clearly a guardian placed by the sorcerer. It lumbered towards them, its massive fists clenching, ready to crush.

"Okay, new plan!" Ethan yelled, pulling Mia behind a jagged rock. "That thing looks like it eats rocks for breakfast!"

Mia's mind raced. Her magic wasn't for direct combat. She couldn't knit a sword or a shield that would stand against a creature of that size. But she had other tools. Distraction. Diversion.

"The rabbits!" she exclaimed, pulling out the larger Hopsy-like rabbits she had knitted. She focused, imbuing them with maximum speed and a mischievous spirit. "Ethan, create a diversion! Get its attention!"

Ethan didn't hesitate. He grabbed a handful of loose rocks and began pelting the Golem, shouting to draw its gaze. The Golem roared, turning its attention to Ethan, its red eyes glowing with fury.

As the Golem lumbered towards Ethan, Mia released the knitted rabbits. They darted out from behind the rock, a flurry of brown and white fur, their knitted legs a blur of motion. They zipped between the Golem's legs, hopped onto its massive feet, and even attempted to climb its rocky back, their tiny knitted paws scrabbling at its rough surface.

The Golem, unused to such small, agile attackers, roared in frustration. It tried to stomp on them, but the rabbits were too fast, too nimble, darting out of the way at the last second. They were a chaotic, furry whirlwind, completely disorienting the massive creature.

"Now!" Mia yelled, pulling out her magical rope. She focused, willing it to extend, to wrap around the Golem's legs. The rope shot out, coiling around the Golem's ankles, tightening with magical force.

The Golem stumbled, its massive weight shifting precariously. It roared again, trying to pull free, but the rope held firm, its unbreakable strength defying the Golem's immense power. Mia then focused on the net, willing it to expand, to ensnare the creature. The net billowed out, light as air, then settled over the Golem, wrapping around its torso and arms, pinning them to its sides.

The Golem thrashed, a trapped beast, its red eyes glowing with impotent rage. But it was ensnared, unable to move, unable to attack.

"Nice work, Weaver!" Ethan cheered, running back to Mia, breathless but exhilarated. "That was brilliant!"

Mia, panting slightly from the exertion of maintaining the magical hold, grinned. "Teamwork. And a lot of yarn."

They quickly moved past the trapped Golem, leaving it to struggle against its magical bonds. As they put distance between themselves and the guardian, Mia released the magic, and the rope and net retracted, leaving the Golem to collapse into a pile of inert rocks and roots, its red eyes fading.

The encounter, though terrifying, had solidified their resolve. Mia's magic was indeed powerful, capable of more than she had imagined. And Ethan's quick thinking and unwavering support were invaluable. They were a team, a formidable duo against the forces of darkness.

As they climbed higher into the foothills, the air grew thinner, colder, and the castle on the peak loomed larger, more menacing. Its dark stone walls seemed to absorb the light, and a perpetual storm cloud swirled around its tallest tower, a dark, bruised eye in the sky. They could almost feel the oppressive magic emanating from it, a heavy weight that pressed down on their spirits.

They knew their next challenge would be the most formidable yet: infiltrating the dragon's keep, rescuing Queen Sasha, and confronting the mighty Dreadwing and the dark sorcerer. The journey had been long, filled with wonders and dangers, but they were closer than ever. The threads of their quest, once so tangled and uncertain, were now unraveling, leading them directly to the heart of Solara's suffering. The final act of their impossible adventure was about to begin.

Chapter 6: The Fabric of Deception

The castle of Dreadwing loomed before them, a jagged scar against the bruised, violet sky of Solara. Its dark stone walls seemed to absorb the very light, and a perpetual storm cloud swirled around its tallest tower, a dark, bruised eye in the sky, occasionally spitting flashes of dark lightning. The air grew colder, heavier, thick with an oppressive magic that pressed down on their spirits, a palpable weight of despair and malevolence. The silence here was absolute, broken only by the mournful whispers of the wind, carrying with it the faint, unsettling scent of ozone and something ancient, something rotten.

Mia shivered, pulling her shimmering cloak tighter around her. Despite its magical warmth, a chill seeped into her bones, a cold dread that had nothing to do with the temperature. This was it. The heart of the darkness. The source of Solara's suffering. The place where Queen Sasha was held captive.

Ethan stood beside her, his hand resting on the hilt of a small, utilitarian knife he'd packed, a gesture of comfort and readiness more than actual defense. His face was grim, but his eyes, though shadowed with apprehension, held a fierce determination. "Okay," he said, his voice low, almost a whisper against the wind. "This is it. The dragon's keep."

Hopsy, perched on Mia's shoulder, twitched its nose nervously, its button eyes fixed on the ominous fortress. The knitted birds, usually so lively, were silent, huddled on Mia's backpack, their tiny forms almost invisible against the dark fabric. Bean and Bear, sensing the immense danger, pressed close to their humans, their low growls a constant rumble in their chests, their fur bristling. Their animal instincts screamed danger, but their loyalty kept them rooted beside Mia and Ethan.

They found a sheltered outcrop of rock, partially hidden by skeletal, thorny bushes, from which they could observe the castle. It was a formidable fortress, designed for defense. High, unscalable walls, battlements lined with what looked like shadowy figures – guards, perhaps, or animated constructs. The main gate was a massive, iron-bound slab of dark wood, seemingly impenetrable. And then there was Dreadwing.

The mighty dragon was a colossal beast, its scales like obsidian, reflecting the bruised sky in dull, malevolent glints. It wasn't perched atop the tower as Mia had initially imagined; instead, it circled the castle, a dark, winged sentinel, its immense shadow sweeping across the battlements with terrifying regularity. Its roars, when they came, were not the distant echoes they had heard in Newark, but guttural, earth-shaking bellows that vibrated through the very ground, sending tremors of fear through Mia's body. Its eyes, when they caught the light, glowed with an infernal, crimson fire, sweeping the landscape below for any sign of intrusion.

"That's… a lot bigger than I imagined," Ethan breathed, his voice tight with awe and dread. "And a lot more active."

Mia nodded, her gaze fixed on the circling beast. A direct confrontation was suicide. Her magic, while powerful, was not for brute force. She couldn't knit a weapon that would fell a creature of Dreadwing's size and power. They needed a plan. A clever strategy. And Mia's unique abilities were their only hope.

They spent hours observing, huddled behind the rocks, the biting wind whipping around them. Ethan, with his engineer's eye for detail, noted the dragon's patrol patterns, the frequency of the shadowy guards' rounds, the subtle shifts in the castle's magical defenses. Mia, meanwhile, focused on the castle's architecture, imagining pathways, hidden entrances, weak points. She felt the oppressive magic emanating from the fortress, a dark, heavy energy that seemed to drain the light from the air.

"The main gate is out," Ethan stated definitively. "And those walls are too high, even with your rope. We'd be exposed for too long."

"What about a hidden entrance?" Mia mused, tracing a finger over a section of the castle wall on Elara Vance's map that seemed to indicate a less fortified side. "Or a way to get inside without being seen?"

"That's where your disguises come in," Ethan said, a flicker of hope in his eyes. "If we can look like one of them, we might be able to walk right in."

The idea was audacious, terrifying, and their best shot. Mia pulled out her needles and a skein of dark, coarse yarn. "What do the guards look like?" she asked, her mind already racing, visualizing the transformation.

Ethan described them: tall, gaunt figures, cloaked in dark, heavy robes, their faces obscured by deep hoods. They carried long, hooked staffs that crackled with faint, dark energy. "They move like shadows," he added. "Almost no sound."

Mia began to knit, her fingers flying, a fierce concentration on her face. She focused on the essence of the guards: *shadow, silence, imposing presence.* The yarn seemed to darken further under her touch, becoming impossibly dense, yet strangely light. She knitted two cloaks, large and flowing, imbued with the magic of concealment and mimicry. As she finished the last stitch, the cloaks shimmered, their fabric shifting, their colors deepening to an inky black that seemed to absorb all light. They felt heavy, yet moved with an unnatural fluidity.

She then knitted two pairs of boots, soft-soled and silent, and two sets of gloves that would extend up their arms, completing the illusion. For the staffs, she knitted long, rigid rods from a darker, almost metallic-looking yarn, focusing on *strength and a faint, crackling energy.* The staffs, once finished, felt surprisingly solid, and a faint, almost imperceptible hum emanated from them, a whisper of dark magic.

"Try them on," Mia instructed, her voice a little hoarse from concentration.

They donned the knitted disguises. The cloaks settled around them, instantly making them feel taller, more imposing. The hoods cast deep shadows over their faces. The boots were silent on the ground. When Ethan picked up his knitted staff, a faint, dark energy seemed to crackle around it, just as he had described.

"This is… unnerving," Ethan muttered, his voice muffled by the hood. He looked at his reflection in a pool of water, a shadowy, ominous figure staring back. "I look like I belong here."

"That's the idea," Mia replied, her own voice sounding deeper, more resonant through the cloak. She felt a strange detachment, as if she had shed her own identity and become something else entirely. It was a powerful, unsettling sensation.

They waited until the twin moons were high in the sky, casting long, distorted shadows across the desolate landscape. Dreadwing was circling, its roars echoing through the night, but its patrols seemed to be less frequent, its attention perhaps dulled by the late hour. This was their window.

"Alright," Ethan whispered, pulling his hood further down. "Remember the plan. Stick to the shadows. Don't make a sound. And if anything goes wrong, Mia, you use your magic to create a diversion. A big one."

Mia nodded, her heart pounding. She had a few more knitted rabbits, imbued with extra speed and a chaotic energy, ready in her bag. She also had her knitted birds, silent and watchful.

They began their approach, moving slowly, deliberately, their camouflaged cloaks making them almost invisible against the dark, jagged rocks. Bean and Bear, surprisingly, seemed to understand the need for stealth. Bean walked close to Mia's heels, her usual playful energy subdued, while Bear, his massive frame moving with surprising grace, padded silently beside Ethan, his golden fur blending into the shadows. Hopsy remained perched on Mia's shoulder, a tiny, silent observer.

They reached the base of the castle walls, a sheer, dark expanse that seemed to stretch endlessly upwards. They followed the less fortified section Ethan had identified, a crumbling service entrance partially obscured by overgrown, thorny vines. It was a narrow, dark opening, barely wide enough for them to squeeze through.

As they approached, a shadowy guard emerged from the gloom, its hooked staff held loosely, its head tilted as if listening to the wind. It was patrolling the entrance.

"Stay still," Ethan whispered, pulling Mia further into the shadows.

Mia held her breath, her hand resting on the knitted rabbits in her bag. The guard was close, its dark robes blending almost perfectly with the stone. Its movements were slow, methodical, almost robotic.

Suddenly, a low, guttural growl emanated from Bear. It was barely audible, a deep rumble of warning, but it was enough. The guard stiffened, its head snapping towards their hiding spot.

"Now!" Ethan hissed.

Mia didn't hesitate. She pulled out a handful of knitted rabbits, imbued them with a frantic, chaotic energy, and flung them towards the guard. The rabbits hit the ground, instantly coming to life, a flurry of brown and white fur. They darted between the guard's legs, hopped onto its feet, and began to climb its robes, scrabbling at its dark fabric, their tiny knitted paws making surprisingly loud thumps.

The guard let out a guttural sound, a strange, rasping noise that was not quite human. It stumbled, flailing its staff, trying to swat away the furry attackers. It was completely disoriented, its methodical patrol broken by the unexpected assault.

"Go!" Mia urged.

They slipped past the distracted guard, squeezing through the narrow service entrance. The passage was dark, damp, and smelled of stale air and ancient stone. They moved quickly, their silent boots barely disturbing the dust on the floor. The sounds of the struggling guard faded behind them.

They found themselves in a labyrinthine network of dimly lit corridors. The castle was a maze, its passages twisting and turning, leading them deeper into its oppressive heart. The walls were rough-hewn stone, devoid of decoration, and the air grew colder, heavier, filled with a subtle, unpleasant hum that seemed to vibrate in their teeth.

Mia's knitted birds proved invaluable here. She sent them ahead, their tiny forms flitting through the darkness, returning with silent signals – a clear path, a dead end, a patrolling guard. They were their eyes and ears in the oppressive gloom.

They encountered more guards, shadowy figures patrolling the corridors with silent, methodical movements. Mia's disguises held firm. They walked past several of them, their hoods pulled low, their knitted staffs held loosely, mimicking the guards' posture. The guards seemed to sense nothing amiss, their vacant gazes sweeping over them without recognition. It was a terrifying gamble, relying on the magic of her knitting to deceive the very guardians of the dark sorcerer.

One time, they nearly blundered into a group of three guards huddled in a small alcove, their guttural voices echoing in the narrow passage. Mia's knitted birds, sent ahead, had returned with frantic flutters, warning them. Mia quickly pulled out a handful of knitted mice, imbuing them with a squeaky, scurrying energy. She flung them down a side corridor, and the mice instantly came to life, scurrying and squeaking loudly, drawing the guards' attention. The guards, startled, turned and pursued the illusory rodents, allowing Mia and Ethan to slip past unnoticed.

The deeper they went, the more oppressive the magic became. It was a dark, suffocating presence, a tangible weight that seemed to drain their energy, to whisper doubts into their minds. Mia felt her own magic, the warmth of her needles, struggling against it, a faint, defiant glow against the encroaching darkness.

They passed through what looked like an old torture chamber, its rusted implements hanging silently from the walls, casting grotesque shadows in the dim light. The air here was heavy with the stench of fear and despair. Mia shuddered, pulling her cloak tighter. Queen Sasha was in this place. She had to be.

Finally, after what felt like an eternity of silent, tense movement, they reached a large, circular chamber. In the center, a massive spiral staircase wound upwards, disappearing into the darkness above. This had to be the way to the tower.

But the chamber was not empty. Several shadowy guards stood sentinel around the base of the staircase, their staffs held at the ready. And in the center of the room, a figure stood, cloaked in robes even darker than the guards', radiating an aura of immense, malevolent power.

The dark sorcerer.

He was tall and gaunt, his face hidden in the depths of his hood, but Mia could feel his gaze, a cold, piercing presence that seemed to strip away her defenses. He was clearly waiting. He knew they were coming.

"This is it," Ethan whispered, his hand tightening on Mia's.

Mia's mind raced. They couldn't fight him directly. His power was too great. But she had her magic. And she had her wits.

She had an idea. A desperate, audacious idea.

"Ethan," she whispered, "I need you to create a distraction. The biggest one you can. Get his attention, just for a few seconds."

Ethan nodded, his eyes fixed on the sorcerer. "What are you going to do?"

"I'm going to knit us a way out," Mia replied, her voice firm, a new resolve hardening in her eyes. "A grand illusion. And then we go for the queen."

She pulled out a large skein of shimmering, almost iridescent yarn, the kind she used for her most elaborate transformations. She focused, not on a physical object, but on a sensation, an overwhelming sensory overload.

"Ready?" she asked Ethan.

He took a deep breath. "Ready."

With a sudden, powerful yell, Ethan stepped out from behind their cover, throwing a handful of rocks at the sorcerer. "Hey, ugly! Looking for someone?"

The sorcerer's head snapped towards Ethan, his hidden face radiating pure, cold fury. The guards immediately moved, staffs raised, ready to attack.

In that precious moment of distraction, Mia acted. Her fingers flew, a blur of motion, her rosewood needles humming with an almost frantic energy. She poured all her will, all her magic, into the yarn, weaving a grand illusion, a tapestry of deception.

She knitted a sudden, blinding flash of light, a burst of pure, white energy that erupted from her hands, momentarily engulfing the chamber. The sorcerer and his guards cried out, shielding their eyes, disoriented by the unexpected brilliance.

Then, as the light faded, a new illusion took hold. The chamber seemed to dissolve, replaced by a swirling vortex of vibrant, chaotic colors – the same disorienting kaleidoscope they had experienced when crossing the threshold into Solara. The air filled with a cacophony of impossible sounds: thunderous roars, piercing screams, the clash of unseen battles, and the mournful wail of a thousand tormented souls. The very ground seemed to tremble beneath their feet, as if the castle itself was tearing apart.

It was a sensory overload, a full-immersion illusion designed to overwhelm and disorient. The sorcerer and his guards staggered, clutching their heads, their dark magic struggling against the sheer, chaotic power of Mia's creation. They were lost in the illusion, trapped in a nightmare of Mia's making.

"Now!" Mia yelled, grabbing Ethan's hand.

They dashed towards the spiral staircase, Bean and Bear scrambling behind them. The illusion held, the chamber still a swirling vortex of chaos, giving them precious seconds. They began to ascend the staircase, its stone steps cold and worn beneath their feet, winding upwards into the inky blackness of the tower.

The air grew colder, heavier, with every step. The oppressive magic intensified, a suffocating presence that seemed to sap their strength, to whisper doubts into their minds. Mia felt her own magic, the warmth of her needles, struggling against it, a faint, defiant glow against the encroaching darkness. But she pushed through, her focus unwavering. Queen Sasha was at the top.

As they climbed, the sounds of the illusion faded behind them, replaced by the ominous silence of the tower, broken only by their own ragged breaths and the soft padding of the dogs' paws. The higher they went, the more Mia could feel the presence of Dreadwing, a vast, ancient power that radiated from the very top of the tower, a primal, slumbering force.

The staircase seemed endless, spiraling upwards into the gloom. Mia's legs ached, her lungs burned, but she pushed on, driven by a fierce determination. Ethan, despite his own fatigue, kept pace, his hand a steady presence at her back.

Finally, after what felt like an eternity, the staircase ended. They emerged onto a circular platform, open to the elements. The air here was frigid, biting, and the wind howled around them, carrying the scent of ozone and something else – something reptilian, ancient, and undeniably dangerous.

And there it was. The top of the tower.

It was a massive, circular chamber, open to the elements, its walls crumbling, its floor scarred and blackened. In the center, a colossal nest of jagged rocks and twisted metal, lay Dreadwing.

The dragon was even more immense up close, a mountain of obsidian scales, its massive head resting on its coiled body. It was slumbering, its breathing a low, rumbling sound that vibrated through the stone floor. Its eyes were closed, but even in sleep, it radiated an aura of immense power, a primal, dangerous force.

And there, chained to a crumbling pillar at the far end of the chamber, was a figure. Small, frail, cloaked in tattered white robes.

Queen Sasha.

She was barely visible, her head bowed, her body slumped against the pillar, but Mia knew it was her. The queen, waiting for rescue.

Mia looked at Ethan. He nodded, his eyes fixed on the dragon, then on the queen. The final challenge.

They moved slowly, carefully, their silent boots
barely disturbing the dust on the floor. The wind
whipped around them, threatening to expose them,
but Mia's cloak held firm, its chameleon magic
making them almost invisible against the crumbling
stone.

They reached the edge of the chamber, hidden
behind a large, fallen block of stone. Dreadwing
stirred, a low rumble emanating from its chest, its
massive head shifting. Mia froze, her heart
hammering. It was still asleep.

"Okay," Ethan whispered, his voice barely audible
above the wind. "How do we get to her without
waking that thing?"

Mia looked at the dragon, then at the queen. Her
magic wasn't for direct combat. But she had other
tools. Distraction. Deception. And perhaps… a
lullaby.

She pulled out a skein of soft, shimmering silver
yarn, the kind she used for her most delicate,
ethereal creations. She focused, not on a physical
object, but on a sound, a melody. A soothing,
enchanting melody.

She began to knit. Her fingers moved with a quiet
urgency, weaving the silver yarn into a delicate,

almost invisible thread. As she knitted, a faint, ethereal melody began to fill the air, a soft, enchanting lullaby that seemed to float on the wind, weaving itself around the slumbering dragon.

The melody was pure, beautiful, filled with a gentle magic that soothed and calmed. Dreadwing stirred again, its massive head lifting slightly, its eyes still closed. The lullaby intensified, wrapping around the beast, pulling it deeper into slumber. The dragon sighed, a long, rumbling exhalation, and its head settled back onto its coiled body, its breathing deepening, becoming slower, more regular. It was falling into a deeper sleep, enchanted by Mia's magical song.

"It's working," Ethan breathed, his eyes wide with awe.

"Go," Mia urged, her voice soft, her focus unwavering on the lullaby. "Get the queen. I'll keep him asleep."

Ethan nodded, and with a silent prayer, he moved. He crept across the chamber, his movements slow and deliberate, his eyes fixed on the slumbering dragon. Bear, ever watchful, padded silently beside him, his massive frame a shadow in the dim light. Bean, too, moved with surprising stealth, a tiny, determined shadow.

Mia continued to knit, the silver yarn flowing through her fingers, the lullaby weaving itself into the very fabric of the air, holding the mighty dragon in its enchanting embrace. She could feel the immense power of the beast, a raw, untamed force, but her magic, soft and subtle, was holding it at bay.

Ethan reached Queen Sasha. Her chains were thick, made of dark, magically reinforced iron. He tried to pull at them, but they held firm.

"Mia!" he whispered, his voice urgent. "The chains! They're enchanted!"

Mia's mind snapped to attention. Enchanted chains. Her magic could unravel, could transform. She shifted her focus from the lullaby, though she kept a faint thread of it going, and poured her will into a new creation.

She pulled out a skein of fine, almost invisible yarn, focusing on *unraveling, dissolving, breaking bonds*. Her fingers flew, weaving a delicate, almost invisible thread. She flung the thread towards Ethan, willing it to wrap around the chains.

The thread shot out, a shimmering silver line in the gloom, wrapping itself around Queen Sasha's chains. As it touched the dark iron, the chains began to shimmer, then to glow faintly, their dark magic struggling against Mia's unraveling spell. The iron began to soften, to twist, to dissolve, its links weakening, then crumbling into dust.

Queen Sasha stirred, her head lifting slowly, her eyes, though clouded with pain and exhaustion, widening in disbelief as she saw the chains dissolving.

"Quickly!" Mia urged, her voice strained from the effort.

Ethan pulled the queen free, supporting her frail form. She was weak, barely able to stand, but her eyes held a flicker of hope.

Suddenly, a low, rumbling growl emanated from Dreadwing. The lullaby was faltering. The dragon was stirring, its massive head lifting, its crimson eyes slowly opening, fixing on Ethan and the queen.

"He's waking up!" Ethan yelled, his voice filled with alarm.

Mia's heart pounded. She couldn't hold the lullaby much longer. She had to act.

She pulled out a large skein of bright, vibrant yarn, her mind racing. She couldn't fight the dragon, but she could distract it. She could create a diversion so grand, so overwhelming, that it would buy them precious seconds.

She began to knit furiously, her fingers a blur. She focused on *chaos, light, sound, overwhelming sensory input.* She knitted a massive, shimmering illusion, a dazzling display of light and sound that erupted from her hands, engulfing the entire chamber.

The illusion was a riot of color and sound – a thousand tiny, glowing sprites dancing in the air, a cacophony of joyful chirps and melodic singing, a shower of iridescent sparks that rained down from the sky. It was beautiful, overwhelming, and utterly disorienting.

Dreadwing roared, a sound of pure frustration and confusion. Its massive head thrashed, its crimson eyes wide, trying to comprehend the sudden, dazzling assault on its senses. It swiped at the air, its claws tearing through the illusory sprites, but they simply reformed, dancing around its head, chirping and singing with renewed vigor.

"Go! Now!" Mia yelled, her voice strained, the effort of maintaining the illusion draining her.

Ethan, supporting Queen Sasha, half-carried her towards the spiral staircase. Bear, with a powerful surge of protective instinct, positioned himself between them and the dragon, his growl a deep, defiant rumble. Bean, too, darted around Dreadwing's feet, a tiny, furry distraction.

They reached the staircase and began their descent, the sounds of Dreadwing's frustrated roars and the chaotic, beautiful symphony of Mia's illusion fading behind them. Mia maintained the illusion for as long as she could, pouring every ounce of her remaining magic into it, buying them precious moments.

Finally, as they reached the lower levels of the tower, the illusion flickered, then vanished. The silence that followed was deafening, broken only by their ragged breaths and the distant, furious roars of Dreadwing.

They had done it. They had rescued Queen Sasha. But the journey was far from over. They still had to get out of the castle, past the dark sorcerer, and back to the portal. The fabric of deception had held, but the threads of their escape were still tenuous.

Chapter 7: The Grand Descent

The furious roars of Dreadwing echoed from the tower chamber above, a chilling testament to the dragon's rage. Mia could feel the vibrations through the stone steps beneath her feet, a primal tremor that seemed to shake the very foundations of the castle. Her illusion had bought them precious seconds, but she knew it wouldn't hold the mighty beast for long. The silence that followed its fading was deafening, punctuated only by their ragged breaths and the frantic thumping of her own heart.

Ethan, supporting Queen Sasha, half-carried her down the winding spiral staircase. The queen was a frail weight in his arms, her body slumped against his, her tattered white robes clinging to her emaciated frame. Her eyes, though now free of the magical haze that had clouded them, were still wide with pain and exhaustion, flickering with a fragile hope that seemed too delicate for the oppressive darkness of the tower. Every step was a struggle, a testament to her prolonged imprisonment.

"Are you alright, Your Majesty?" Ethan whispered, his voice strained from the exertion.

Queen Sasha managed a weak nod, a faint, almost imperceptible movement. "As well as can be expected, young man," she rasped, her voice thin, like a whisper of dry leaves. "The air… it feels lighter already. Your magic, Weaver… it is truly a gift." She looked at Mia, a flicker of something ancient and knowing in her eyes, a recognition that went beyond mere gratitude.

Mia, still panting from the effort of maintaining the illusion, offered a weak smile. Her magical energy felt drained, a hollow ache behind her eyes, but the sight of the queen, free from her chains, ignited a new spark of determination within her. They had done the impossible. Now, they just had to get out.

The descent felt endless. The spiral staircase seemed to coil downwards into an abyss, each step taking them deeper into the castle's suffocating embrace. The air grew colder, heavier, the oppressive magic intensifying with every turn, a tangible weight that pressed down on their spirits, whispering doubts into their minds. Mia felt her own magic, the warmth of her needles, struggling against it, a faint, defiant glow against the encroaching darkness. It was like swimming against a powerful, unseen current.

Bean and Bear, usually so agile, moved with a newfound caution. Bean whimpered softly, pressing close to Mia's leg, her nose twitching, sensing the malevolent energies that permeated the stone. Bear, his massive frame moving with surprising grace, kept a watchful eye on their surroundings, his low growl a constant rumble in his chest, a deep, protective warning. Hopsy, the knitted rabbit, remained perched on Mia's shoulder, its button eyes wide and alert, its tiny body vibrating with nervous energy. The knitted birds, usually flitting ahead, now huddled silently on Mia's backpack, their tiny forms almost invisible against the dark fabric, sensing the imminent danger.

As they reached the lower levels of the tower, the distant roars of Dreadwing began to fade, replaced by a new, more immediate threat. A faint, guttural murmur echoed from below, growing steadily louder. The dark sorcerer. He would know. He would be waiting.

"They're coming," Ethan whispered, his grip on Queen Sasha tightening. "He'll have sent more guards."

Mia's mind raced, her fingers already twitching, anticipating the need to knit. Her disguises were likely compromised, their chameleon cloaks useless if the sorcerer knew they were inside. They needed a new strategy, a way to navigate the labyrinthine corridors with a weakened queen and a furious sorcerer on their heels.

They reached the bottom of the spiral staircase and emerged into the large, circular chamber they had passed through earlier. The illusion Mia had created was gone, leaving behind only the oppressive gloom and the cold, unyielding stone. The chamber was empty, but the air crackled with a residual dark energy, a lingering malevolence that spoke of the sorcerer's recent presence.

Suddenly, from the shadows of a side corridor, a figure emerged. Tall, gaunt, cloaked in robes even darker than the guards', radiating an aura of immense, malevolent power. The dark sorcerer. He stood there, his face hidden in the depths of his hood, but Mia could feel his gaze, a cold, piercing presence that seemed to strip away her defenses, to see into her very soul. He was not alone. Behind him, a dozen shadowy guards emerged, their hooked staffs held at the ready, their vacant eyes fixed on Mia, Ethan, and the queen.

"So, the little Weaver finally shows herself," the sorcerer's voice was a dry, rasping hiss, devoid of emotion, yet filled with a chilling power that seemed to vibrate through the very stone. "And you bring my prize with you. Foolish. Did you truly think you could escape Dreadwing's keep?"

"Let her go!" Ethan yelled, stepping slightly in front of Mia and Queen Sasha, a defiant, protective stance.

The sorcerer chuckled, a sound like dry leaves skittering across stone. "Foolish boy. You are but a distraction. The Weaver is mine. Her magic will serve my will, and Solara will truly fall into darkness." He raised a hand, and the guards advanced, their staffs crackling with dark energy.

Mia's heart hammered. She couldn't fight them. Not directly. Not with Queen Sasha so weak. She needed a diversion, something massive, something that would buy them enough time to escape the chamber.

She pulled out a large skein of vibrant, fiery orange yarn, her mind racing, her fingers a blur. She focused on *heat, light, overwhelming sensory input, chaos*. She poured every ounce of her remaining magical energy into the yarn, weaving a grand, terrifying illusion.

"Ethan! Get ready!" she yelled.

As the guards advanced, Mia flung the knitted yarn forward. It exploded in a burst of brilliant, searing light, momentarily blinding everyone in the chamber. Then, the illusion solidified. The chamber seemed to erupt in a raging inferno. Walls of fire, impossibly real, sprang up around them, licking at the stone, casting dancing, grotesque shadows. The air filled with the roar of flames, the crackle of burning wood, and the acrid smell of smoke. The heat was intense, suffocating, even though Mia knew it was not real.

The guards cried out, stumbling back, shielding their faces, their dark robes seemingly singed by the illusory flames. Even the sorcerer recoiled, his hood momentarily flaring as he instinctively raised a hand to ward off the heat. He was powerful, but even he was susceptible to the raw, chaotic power of Mia's illusion.

"Go! Now!" Mia urged, grabbing Ethan's arm.

Ethan, supporting Queen Sasha, dashed towards a side corridor, one they had noted earlier as a potential escape route. Bear, with a powerful surge of protective instinct, positioned himself between them and the illusion, his growl a deep, defiant rumble, as if challenging the very flames. Bean, too, darted around their feet, a tiny, determined shadow.

They slipped into the corridor, the roar of the illusory fire fading behind them, replaced by the muffled shouts of the disoriented guards and the sorcerer's furious, rasping curses. Mia maintained the illusion for as long as she could, pouring every ounce of her remaining magic into it, buying them precious moments. She could feel the drain, the exhaustion creeping into her bones, but she pushed through, her focus unwavering.

The corridor was narrow, twisting, and plunged into near-total darkness. Mia's knitted birds, sent ahead, returned with frantic flutters, warning them of dead ends and patrolling guards. They were their eyes and ears in the oppressive gloom. Queen Sasha, though weak, occasionally offered a whispered direction, her ancient knowledge of the castle's layout proving invaluable. "Left here, young ones… the old servants' passage… it leads to the lower dungeons."

The lower dungeons. Mia shuddered. The air grew colder, damper, thick with the stench of mildew and despair. Rusted iron bars lined the walls, leading to empty, echoing cells. The oppressive magic here was almost unbearable, a tangible weight that pressed down on their spirits, whispering doubts into their minds, trying to sap their will. Mia felt her own magic, the warmth of her needles, struggling against it, a faint, defiant glow against the encroaching darkness. It was a constant, draining battle of wills.

They encountered more guards, shadowy figures patrolling the corridors with silent, methodical movements. Their disguises, though still functional, were now a liability. The sorcerer would have alerted them, given them descriptions. They couldn't rely on simply walking past them.

"New plan," Mia whispered to Ethan as they heard the rhythmic thud of approaching footsteps. "We need to create diversions. Lots of them. And we need to be silent."

She pulled out a handful of her knitted mice, imbuing them with a squeaky, scurrying energy. She flung them down a side corridor, and the mice instantly came to life, scurrying and squeaking loudly, drawing the guards' attention. The guards, startled, turned and pursued the illusory rodents, their staffs clattering against the stone, allowing Mia and Ethan to slip past unnoticed.

For another group of guards blocking a crucial intersection, Mia knitted a large, shimmering illusion of a collapsing wall. The stone seemed to crack and crumble, dust billowed, and the sound of falling debris echoed through the corridor. The guards cried out in alarm, scrambling to avoid the non-existent collapse, giving Mia and Ethan a clear path.

But the magic was taking its toll. Mia's head throbbed, her vision blurred at the edges, and her hands, usually so nimble, trembled with fatigue. The rosewood needles, though still warm, felt heavier, as if resisting her will. She was pushing her limits, drawing on reserves she didn't know she possessed.

"You're doing great, Mia," Ethan whispered, his voice filled with concern, but also immense pride. He shifted Queen Sasha's weight, trying to ease her discomfort. "Just a little further."

Queen Sasha, though mostly silent, occasionally offered a word of encouragement, her voice frail but clear. "The Weaver… her spirit is strong. Solara needs her light." Her words, though few, were a powerful reminder of the stakes, of the land waiting for its queen, for its balance to be restored.

They moved deeper into the castle's bowels, navigating through abandoned storerooms filled with cobwebs and decaying supplies, through damp, echoing cisterns where unseen water dripped. The air grew thick with a cloying, stagnant smell, and the oppressive magic seemed to press in on them from all sides, a suffocating blanket of despair. Mia felt a growing sense of claustrophobia, the walls closing in, the darkness threatening to consume them.

Bear, usually so placid, was becoming increasingly agitated. He would stop abruptly, his fur bristling, his nose twitching, letting out low, guttural growls at unseen threats. Bean, too, would whine softly, burying her head against Mia's leg, sensing the malevolent energies that permeated the stone.

Suddenly, Bear let out a loud, furious bark, lunging forward. From the shadows, a creature emerged. It was not a guard, but something far more sinister. A shadowy construct, its form shifting and swirling like living smoke, its eyes glowing with a cold, malevolent light. It was clearly a magical guardian, designed to detect and destroy intruders.

"A Shadow Hound!" Queen Sasha gasped, her voice filled with a sudden, sharp fear. "It hunts by magic! It will see through your illusions, Weaver!"

Mia's heart plummeted. A creature that could see through her illusions? This was a direct counter to her primary defense. She couldn't fight it physically, and her magic of deception was useless.

"Mia, run!" Ethan yelled, pushing Queen Sasha behind him, pulling out his small knife, a futile gesture against such a foe.

The Shadow Hound lunged, its smoky form coalescing into jagged claws, its glowing eyes fixed on Mia.

Mia's mind raced, desperate. She couldn't run. Not with Queen Sasha so weak. She had to think of something. Something beyond illusion. Something to physically block it, to contain it.

She pulled out a skein of thick, coarse, dark gray yarn, the kind she used for heavy-duty projects. She focused on *immobility, containment, unbreakable barrier.* Her fingers flew, weaving with a frantic, desperate speed.

She knitted a massive, solid wall. Not an illusion, but a tangible, physical barrier of knitted stone. The yarn seemed to harden, to solidify, forming a thick, impenetrable wall of dark gray, rough-textured fabric that instantly sprang up between them and the Shadow Hound, blocking the corridor.

The Shadow Hound slammed into the knitted wall with a shriek of frustration, its smoky form rippling, trying to pass through. But the wall held firm, its magically reinforced fibers resisting the creature's attempts. It was a physical barrier, not an illusion, and the Shadow Hound, though it could see through magic, could not pass through solid matter.

"It's holding!" Ethan exclaimed, his voice filled with disbelief and relief.

Mia, panting, leaned against the wall, her energy completely depleted. The rosewood needles were cold in her hands, drained of their warmth, their hum silenced. She had pushed herself too far.

"We need to move," she whispered, her voice hoarse. "Before it finds a way around."

They continued their desperate flight, Mia leaning heavily on Ethan, Queen Sasha supported between them. The knitted wall, a temporary reprieve, would not hold forever. They could hear the furious snarls of the Shadow Hound echoing behind them, its attempts to break through the barrier.

They finally reached the service entrance, the narrow, crumbling opening they had used to enter the castle. The air here felt slightly fresher, less oppressive, a faint promise of freedom.

"It's open!" Ethan exclaimed, relief flooding his voice.

But as they approached, a sudden, blinding flash of dark lightning erupted from the opening, followed by a guttural roar. Dreadwing. The dragon was outside, alerted by the commotion, guarding the only apparent exit.

Mia's heart sank. Trapped. Between a Shadow Hound and a dragon.

"There must be another way," Queen Sasha whispered, her voice surprisingly strong, a flicker of her regal determination returning. "The old escape tunnel… beneath the kitchens. It leads to the outer wall, near the western cliffs."

"The kitchens?" Ethan looked around, disoriented. "Where are the kitchens?"

"Follow me," Queen Sasha said, pushing herself upright, her strength momentarily bolstered by the urgency of the situation. She pointed to a small, unassuming archway, almost hidden in the shadows. "It is a secret passage, known only to the royal family and a few trusted servants."

They followed Queen Sasha, their hopes rekindled. The passage was even narrower than the service entrance, barely wide enough for them to squeeze through. It sloped downwards, leading them into the very bowels of the castle. The air here was hot, thick with the lingering scent of old food and something metallic, like burnt magic.

They found themselves in a vast, echoing kitchen, filled with enormous, rusted cooking implements and long, grimy tables. The air was still and stagnant, as if no one had cooked here for centuries.

"The tunnel is behind the main hearth," Queen Sasha directed, pointing to a massive, soot-blackened fireplace.

As they approached, a low, guttural growl echoed from the passage they had just left. The knitted wall had given way. The Shadow Hound was coming.

"Mia, can you knit anything to slow it down?" Ethan asked, his voice urgent.

Mia shook her head, her voice hoarse. "I… I'm drained. The needles are cold." She held them up; they were indeed dull, lifeless, their warmth completely gone. She had pushed her magic beyond its limits.

"Then we run!" Ethan declared. He helped Queen Sasha towards the hearth, pulling at a loose stone.

The stone shifted, revealing a dark, narrow opening. A tunnel.

Just as they were about to enter, the Shadow Hound burst into the kitchen, its smoky form swirling, its glowing eyes fixed on them. It shrieked, a sound of pure malevolence, and lunged.

Bear, with a roar, threw himself forward, placing his massive body between them and the creature. He snarled, snapping at the smoky form, his teeth meeting no resistance, but his sheer presence, his unwavering courage, momentarily startled the Shadow Hound.

"Bear, no!" Ethan cried, but the loyal dog held his ground, buying them precious seconds.

"Go!" Mia yelled, pushing Ethan and Queen Sasha into the tunnel. She hesitated, looking at Bear, her heart breaking.

"Mia! Come on!" Ethan urged, pulling her into the tunnel.

Bear let out another defiant bark, then, with a final, desperate lunge, he snapped at the Shadow Hound, forcing it back for a crucial moment.

They scrambled through the narrow tunnel, the sounds of Bear's growls and the Shadow Hound's furious snarls fading behind them. It was a tight squeeze, dark and claustrophobic, but they pushed through, driven by the desperate need for escape. Queen Sasha, despite her weakness, moved with surprising speed, her knowledge of the passage guiding them.

The tunnel sloped upwards, and soon they could feel a faint breeze, hear the distant howl of the wind. A glimmer of light appeared ahead.

They burst out onto a narrow ledge on the outer wall of the castle, high above the ground. The wind whipped around them, cold and biting, but the air felt clean, free of the oppressive magic of the castle. Below them, the western cliffs dropped away into a dizzying abyss, and beyond, the desolate landscape of Solara stretched into the distance.

Dreadwing was still circling the main gate, its roars echoing across the plains, unaware of their escape from the western side. They had made it out.

Mia looked back at the castle, her heart heavy. Bear. He had sacrificed himself for them. Tears welled in her eyes, hot and stinging.

Ethan put an arm around her, his own face grim. "He bought us time, Mia. He saved us."

Queen Sasha, leaning heavily against the cold stone, looked at the castle, then at Mia. "A brave sacrifice. He will be remembered, Weaver." Her voice was filled with a profound sadness.

They were out of the castle, but they were still deep in enemy territory. The sorcerer would undoubtedly send forces after them. They needed to get back to the forgotten grove, back to the portal, and return Queen Sasha to her people.

Mia looked at her rosewood needles, now cold and lifeless in her hand. Her magic was depleted. She was exhausted, emotionally and physically. But they had the queen. And they had each other. The journey was far from over, but they had taken a crucial step. The threads of their escape were tenuous, but they held. They had to. For Bear. For Solara. For Queen Sasha.

Chapter 8: The Desolate Path

The biting wind on the castle's outer wall was a harsh, cold slap of reality. Below them, the western cliffs plunged into a dizzying abyss, a jagged maw of darkness. Above, the castle loomed, a silent, malevolent sentinel, its dark stone walls still radiating the oppressive magic that had permeated their every step. Dreadwing's furious roars, though distant now, still echoed across the desolate plains, a chilling reminder of the beast they had narrowly escaped. But the most profound silence, the heaviest weight, was the absence of Bear.

Mia leaned against the cold stone, her body trembling, not just from the wind, but from the raw, aching grief that tore at her heart. Bear. Her loyal, gentle giant. He had sacrificed himself, a selfless act of courage that had bought them the precious seconds needed to escape. Tears welled in her eyes, hot and stinging, blurring the desolate landscape before her. His last defiant bark, his final lunge at the Shadow Hound, replayed in her mind, a heartbreaking loop.

Ethan, his own face grim with sorrow, wrapped an arm around her, pulling her close. His touch was a small comfort against the vast emptiness that Bear's absence left. "He bought us time, Mia," he murmured, his voice thick with emotion. "He saved us. We have to make it count."

Queen Sasha, leaning heavily against the cold stone, her frail form swaying in the wind, looked at the castle, then at Mia, her ancient eyes filled with a profound sadness. "A brave sacrifice," she rasped, her voice thin but clear. "He will be remembered, Weaver. His courage will light the path." Her words, though meant to comfort, only deepened Mia's grief. Bear deserved more than to be remembered; he deserved to be here, safe, running free.

Bean, sensing the profound sorrow of her humans, whimpered softly, nudging Mia's leg with her nose, then Ethan's. She looked back at the castle, then at the desolate plains, a silent question in her intelligent eyes. She understood. She mourned.

Mia looked at her rosewood needles, now cold and lifeless in her hand. Her magic was depleted, utterly drained by the frantic escape and the powerful, desperate illusions. The warmth was gone, the subtle hum silenced. They felt like ordinary pieces of wood, incapable of the wonders they had just performed. She was exhausted, emotionally and physically, a hollow ache behind her eyes, a profound weariness that settled deep in her bones. But they had the queen. And they had each other. The journey was far from over, but they had taken a crucial, devastating step.

"We need to move," Ethan said, his voice firm, pulling Mia gently away from the wall. "The sorcerer will know we're out. He'll send forces after us."

Queen Sasha nodded, pushing herself upright with a surprising surge of strength. "Indeed. He will not rest until I am recaptured. And he will be furious." Her gaze swept across the desolate landscape. "We must reach the Whispering Plains. They offer some cover, and lead towards the Sunken Mire, which eventually connects to the ancient path to the portal."

The desolate landscape of Solara stretched before them, a vast expanse of jagged rocks, thorny, skeletal trees, and dry, cracked earth. The twin moons, high in the sky, cast long, distorted shadows, painting the world in shades of violet and ghostly silver. The air was frigid, biting, and the wind howled around them, carrying the scent of ozone and something ancient, something decaying. This was not the vibrant, sapphire forest they had entered; this was a land choked by darkness, its magic twisted and corrupted.

Their pace was slow, hampered by Queen Sasha's weakness and Mia's exhaustion. Ethan, ever the protector, supported the queen, easing her steps, offering her sips of water from his canteen. Mia, though drained, kept a watchful eye on their surroundings, her senses heightened by adrenaline and grief. Bean, usually so energetic, walked close to Mia's heels, her head down, her tail drooping, a silent companion in their shared sorrow. Hopsy, the knitted rabbit, remained perched on Mia's shoulder, its button eyes wide and alert, its tiny body vibrating with nervous energy, sensing the danger that still lurked. The knitted birds, usually flitting ahead, now huddled silently on Mia's backpack, their tiny forms almost invisible against the dark fabric, their usual chirps replaced by a quiet, watchful stillness.

As they walked, the queen began to speak, her voice frail but clear, recounting the tale of her imprisonment. "He came from the Shadowlands, the sorcerer, a creature of pure malevolence. He sought to drain Solara of its light, to twist its magic to his own dark purpose. He knew of the Weaver, of the Heart Weaver, and he feared her power. He imprisoned me, hoping to break the spirit of the land, to sever its connection to the light." She spoke of Dreadwing, a dragon corrupted by the sorcerer's dark magic, forced to serve his will. Her words painted a vivid, terrifying picture of a land suffering, its vibrant magic slowly being choked by the encroaching darkness.

Mia listened, her heart aching for the queen, for Solara. It solidified her resolve. This wasn't just about escaping; it was about restoring. About mending.

They reached the Whispering Plains as dawn approached, painting the horizon in bruised purples and grays. The plains were a vast expanse of tall, withered grasses that rustled with an eerie, whispering sound in the wind, like a thousand hushed voices. It offered some cover, but also a sense of exposure, the open expanse making them feel vulnerable.

"We need to find shelter," Ethan urged, scanning the horizon. "The sorcerer's forces will be searching for us. And we need to rest. Mia, your magic needs to recover."

Mia nodded, her eyelids heavy. The thought of sleeping, even for a few hours, felt like an impossible luxury. But she knew Ethan was right. She couldn't be a Weaver of Light if she was too exhausted to knit.

They found a shallow ravine, its sides lined with gnarled, skeletal trees, offering a modicum of concealment. Mia, despite her exhaustion, tried to knit a small, camouflaged tent, but her needles remained cold, unresponsive. The magic was truly gone, at least for now.

"It's okay," Ethan said gently, seeing her frustration. "We'll just have to rough it. We'll be fine." He pulled out their emergency blanket, a thin, reflective sheet, and draped it over them, trying to conserve what little warmth they had.

They huddled together, Queen Sasha shivering despite the blanket, her frail body radiating cold. Ethan kept watch, his eyes scanning the horizon, his hand never straying far from his knife. Mia tried to rest, but sleep wouldn't come. Her mind replayed Bear's sacrifice, the sorcerer's chilling words, the desperate flight through the castle.

As the sun, a pale, anemic disk in the Solara sky, finally rose, they heard it. The distant thud of hooves, the faint jingle of armor. The sorcerer's forces.

"They're coming," Ethan whispered, his voice grim. "And they're fast."

Mia's heart pounded. Her magic was gone. They were vulnerable.

"We need to move," Queen Sasha urged, her voice gaining a surprising urgency. "The Sunken Mire. It is

treacherous, but it will slow them down. And they
will not expect us to enter it."

The Sunken Mire. The name itself sounded
ominous. But it was their only chance.

They pushed on, Queen Sasha, despite her weakness,
moving with a newfound determination, driven by
the urgency of escape. The Whispering Plains gave
way to a landscape of stagnant, murky pools,
treacherous bogs, and stunted, twisted trees draped
with sickly, glowing moss. The air grew thick with
the stench of decay and sulfur, and a cold, damp
mist clung to the ground, obscuring their vision.

"Stay close," Ethan warned, testing the ground with
his foot before each step. "One wrong move and we
could be swallowed whole."

The mire was a nightmare. The ground was soft and
yielding, threatening to pull them down with every
step. They sank into knee-deep mud, their boots
squelching, their progress agonizingly slow. The mist
made it impossible to see more than a few feet
ahead, and the eerie silence was broken only by the
squelching of their footsteps and the occasional plop
of something unseen in the murky water.

Mia felt a wave of despair wash over her. Her magic
was gone, her body ached, and now they were

trapped in this desolate, dangerous swamp. How could they possibly make it through?

But then, a faint, almost imperceptible warmth spread through her hand. She looked down. Her rosewood needles, clutched in her hand, were glowing faintly, a soft, internal luminescence. The hum was back, faint but undeniable. Her magic was returning. Slowly.

A surge of hope, fierce and bright, ignited within her. She was not powerless. Not yet.

"Ethan," she whispered, her voice hoarse with exhaustion and excitement. "My needles. They're warming up. The magic… it's coming back."

Ethan looked at her, his eyes wide with relief. "Thank the stars! What can you do?"

Mia thought quickly. They needed to move faster, to navigate the mire more safely. And they needed to leave a false trail, to throw off their pursuers.

She pulled out a skein of dark, earthy brown yarn. She focused on *solid ground, safe passage, illusion of movement*. Her fingers, though still trembling, began to knit.

She knitted a series of small, flat, circular pads, imbuing them with the magic of temporary solidification. As she finished each one, she dropped it onto the murky surface of the mire. The pads landed with a soft plop, instantly solidifying the mud beneath them, creating temporary stepping stones.

"Step on these," Mia instructed, her voice gaining strength. "They'll hold our weight, but only for a few seconds. We need to be quick."

They began to move, leaping from one knitted pad to the next, their progress significantly faster. The pads would hold their weight for a brief moment, then dissolve back into the mire, leaving no trace. It was a precarious dance, but it allowed them to navigate the treacherous swamp with surprising speed.

As they moved, Mia also knitted a series of small, ethereal illusions – shimmering figures that resembled them, darting off in different directions, creating false trails. The Shadow Hound might see through illusions, but the guards would be fooled, sending them off on wild goose chases.

The mire was still dangerous, but Mia's returning magic gave them a fighting chance. Bean, sensing the renewed hope, whined softly, her tail giving a tentative wag. Hopsy, the knitted rabbit, seemed to pulse with a faint, inner light, its button eyes fixed on the path ahead.

They heard the sounds of the sorcerer's forces entering the mire – shouts of frustration, the heavy splashing of their boots in the mud, the occasional cry of a guard sinking into a hidden bog. Mia's illusions were working, scattering them, buying them precious time.

As they pushed deeper into the mire, the air grew even thicker, the mist denser, obscuring the path ahead. The stunted trees became more gnarled, their branches twisting into grotesque, skeletal forms. The glowing moss pulsed with a sickly green light, illuminating strange, unseen things in the murky water.

Suddenly, a low, guttural growl echoed from the mist directly ahead. Not a Shadow Hound. Something else. Something larger.

A creature emerged from the mist, its form massive and indistinct, its eyes glowing with a dull, malevolent yellow light. It was a Mire Beast, a monstrous creature of mud and tangled roots, a guardian of the swamp, animated by the dark magic that permeated the land. It lumbered towards them, its massive limbs churning the murky water, its jaws opening to reveal rows of jagged, moss-covered teeth.

"Oh, come on!" Ethan groaned, pulling Queen Sasha behind him. "Another one?"

Mia's needles, though still cool, hummed with a faint energy. Her magic was returning, but slowly. She couldn't knit another wall. Not yet. She needed a different approach.

She looked at Hopsy, then at the knitted birds. Diversion. Chaos.

"Ethan, get its attention!" Mia yelled, pulling out her remaining knitted animals. She imbued them with a frantic, chaotic energy, focusing on *noise, movement, overwhelming sensory input.*

Ethan didn't hesitate. He grabbed a handful of mud and flung it at the Mire Beast, yelling to draw its gaze. The Mire Beast roared, turning its massive head towards Ethan, its yellow eyes glowing with fury.

As the Mire Beast lumbered towards Ethan, Mia released the knitted animals. Hopsy, the rabbits, and the birds darted out from behind them, a flurry of furry and feathered chaos. They zipped between the Mire Beast's legs, hopped onto its massive feet, and even attempted to climb its root-covered body, their tiny knitted paws scrabbling at its rough surface. The birds chirped loudly, fluttering around its head, pecking at its glowing eyes.

The Mire Beast, unused to such small, agile attackers, roared in frustration. It tried to stomp on them, but the knitted creatures were too fast, too nimble, darting out of the way at the last second. They were a chaotic, furry, feathered whirlwind, completely disorienting the massive creature.

"Now!" Mia yelled, pulling out a skein of fine, almost invisible yarn. She focused on *entanglement, binding, slowing.* Her fingers flew, weaving a delicate, yet incredibly strong, web of yarn.

She flung the web towards the Mire Beast. It shot out, a shimmering, almost invisible net, wrapping itself around the creature's limbs, tightening with magical force. The Mire Beast roared, thrashing, trying to pull free, but the web held firm, its magically reinforced fibers resisting the creature's immense power. It was entangled, slowed, unable to move effectively.

"Go!" Mia urged, grabbing Ethan's arm.

They scrambled past the struggling Mire Beast, leaving it to thrash against its magical bonds. The sounds of its furious roars and the frantic chirping of the knitted birds faded behind them as they pushed deeper into the mire.

The Sunken Mire seemed to stretch endlessly, a suffocating, dangerous landscape. But as they pressed on, the mist began to thin, the air grew slightly clearer, and the stunted trees began to give way to more recognizable, albeit still ancient, flora. The stench of decay lessened, replaced by the faint, earthy scent of damp soil.

They were nearing the end of the mire.

Finally, after what felt like an eternity, the treacherous bogs gave way to solid ground. They emerged onto a narrow, overgrown path, flanked by ancient, moss-covered trees whose branches intertwined overhead, forming a natural archway. This was the ancient path Queen Sasha had spoken of, the one leading towards the portal.

They collapsed onto the dry ground, panting, exhausted, but alive. Mia's needles, though still cool, now held a faint, steady warmth, their hum a quiet, comforting presence. Her magic was slowly but surely returning, a testament to her resilience.

"We made it," Ethan breathed, collapsing beside her, his body aching.

Queen Sasha, though still frail, managed a small, tired smile. "Indeed. The Mire Beast will hold them for a time. But the sorcerer will not give up. We must continue."

Mia looked at the path ahead. It was overgrown, winding, but it felt different from the oppressive darkness of the castle, or the suffocating gloom of the mire. It felt… hopeful. A path towards light.

They rested for a short while, gathering their strength. Mia allowed herself a moment to mourn Bear, the tears flowing freely now, a quiet, cleansing release. She knew his sacrifice would not be in vain. They would honor his memory by succeeding.

As they prepared to move, Mia felt a gentle nudge against her leg. Bean. The little terrier mix looked up at her, her eyes filled with a quiet understanding, a shared grief, but also a silent promise of continued loyalty. Mia knelt, wrapping her arms around Bean, burying her face in her soft fur. They were all they had left.

The Sunken Mire was behind them, a treacherous obstacle overcome. But the journey was far from over. They were still deep in Solara, pursued by a powerful sorcerer and his forces. They needed to reach the portal, to return Queen Sasha to her people, and to restore the balance to this suffering land. The desolate path stretched before them, leading them towards an uncertain future, but also towards the hope of a new dawn for Solara. The threads of their quest, though frayed, still held, leading them onward.

Chapter 9: The Ancient Path and the Sorcerer's Shadow

The ancient path was a welcome reprieve after the suffocating gloom of the Sunken Mire. It was narrow and overgrown, flanked by towering, moss-covered trees whose branches intertwined overhead, forming a natural archway that filtered the bruised light of Solara into dappled patterns on the forest floor. The air here was cleaner, fresher, carrying the faint, earthy scent of damp soil and the sweet, almost forgotten perfume of unseen blossoms. It felt different from the castle's oppressive darkness or the mire's stagnant decay; it felt… hopeful. A path towards light, towards home.

They collapsed onto the dry ground, panting, exhausted, but alive. Mia's needles, though still cool, now held a faint, steady warmth, their hum a quiet, comforting presence against her palm. Her magic was slowly but surely returning, a testament to her resilience, a flicker of light in the encroaching darkness.

"We made it," Ethan breathed, collapsing beside her, his body aching, his face streaked with mud and sweat, but his eyes alight with relief. He pulled a water bottle from his pack, offering it first to Queen Sasha, then to Mia.

Queen Sasha, though still frail, managed a small, tired smile as she took a grateful sip. "Indeed. The Mire Beast will hold them for a time. But the sorcerer will not give up. He will be relentless. We must continue." Her voice, though still thin, carried a renewed strength, a flicker of her regal determination returning.

Mia allowed herself a moment to mourn Bear, the tears flowing freely now, a quiet, cleansing release. She buried her face in Bean's soft fur, the little terrier mix whimpering softly, her eyes filled with a quiet understanding, a shared grief, but also a silent promise of continued loyalty. Bear's sacrifice would not be in vain. They would honor his memory by succeeding, by bringing Queen Sasha home, by restoring Solara.

After a short rest, they pushed on. The ancient path wound deeper into the forest, its twists and turns seeming to follow an unseen logic. The trees here were truly ancient, their massive trunks scarred with the marks of time, their branches reaching towards the twin moons like gnarled, supplicating hands. Strange, glowing fungi clung to their bark, casting soft, ethereal lights that pulsed with a gentle rhythm, illuminating their way.

As they walked, Queen Sasha, bolstered by the rest and the clean air, began to speak more, her voice gaining strength with every word. She recounted the history of Solara, a land once vibrant with magic, its people living in harmony with the natural world, guided by the Heart Weavers, a lineage of magic-users whose craft maintained the balance of the land.

"The Heart Weavers," she explained, her gaze falling on Mia's knitting needles, "were the soul of Solara. They did not wield destructive power, but rather the power of creation, of mending, of weaving life and light into being. They spun the very threads of reality, ensuring our world remained vibrant and whole. Your magic, Weaver, is a reflection of that ancient lineage."

Mia listened, fascinated. It explained the profound connection she felt to her needles, the way the magic flowed so naturally. It was not just a random gift; it was a legacy.

Queen Sasha then spoke of the sorcerer, his name, a chilling whisper, was Malakor. "He was once a respected scholar, obsessed with the ancient magics of Solara. But he sought power, not balance. He delved into forbidden arts, drawing energy from the

Shadowlands, twisting the very essence of creation to his malevolent will. He corrupted Dreadwing, binding the noble dragon to his service, and imprisoned me, hoping to sever Solara's connection to the Heart Weavers, to plunge our land into eternal darkness."

Her words painted a vivid, terrifying picture of Malakor's ambition, his ruthless pursuit of power. He feared the Weaver, the Queen explained, because the Weaver's magic was the antithesis of his own. His sought to unravel; hers sought to mend.

As the queen spoke, Mia felt her own magic returning, not just as a faint hum, but as a steady, vibrant pulse in her needles. The warmth spread from her hands, up her arms, filling her with a renewed sense of energy and purpose. She could feel the latent power, ready to be called upon.

"My magic is coming back, full strength," Mia whispered to Ethan, her eyes bright. "I can feel it."

Ethan grinned, a flash of his old, easygoing charm. "Good. Because I have a feeling we're going to need it."

He was right. As they continued along the ancient path, the sounds of pursuit began to grow louder. The distant shouts of the sorcerer's guards, the faint jingle of armor, the heavy thud of their boots on the forest floor. Malakor was relentless. He would not give up.

"They're gaining on us," Ethan said, his voice grim. "We need to find a way to slow them down, or lose them entirely."

Mia looked around. The path was narrow, winding. Perfect for an ambush, or a diversion.

"I have an idea," she said, pulling out a skein of thick, dark green yarn. "A physical barrier. Something they can't just walk through."

She began to knit furiously, her fingers a blur. She focused on *growth, entanglement, impenetrable barrier.* She knitted a massive, sprawling thicket of thorny vines, imbued with rapid growth and an aggressive, binding magic.

As she finished, she flung the knitted yarn behind them. It landed on the path, instantly sprouting into a dense, thorny thicket, its vines twisting and growing with impossible speed, forming an impenetrable wall of sharp, barbed branches that completely blocked the path. The thorns glowed faintly with a malevolent green light, and any attempt to touch them would result in a painful, binding grip.

They heard the shouts of the guards as they slammed into the thorny barrier, their cries of frustration echoing through the forest. The thicket held, its magic resisting their attempts to cut or burn through it.

"That should buy us some time," Mia said, panting slightly, her magic already feeling stronger than before.

They pushed on, the sounds of the struggling guards fading behind them. But Malakor was not easily deterred. A new sound began to echo through the forest, a low, guttural snarl that Mia recognized with a chill of dread.

"Shadow Hounds," Queen Sasha whispered, her eyes wide with fear. "He has sent them. They will track us by magic. They will see through your illusions, Weaver."

Mia's heart pounded. Her physical barrier would hold the guards, but the Shadow Hounds were different. They were creatures of magic, capable of bypassing physical obstacles and seeing through deception. They would find them.

"We need to go off the path," Mia decided, looking into the dense, ancient forest. "They'll expect us to stay on the trail. We need to disappear."

Ethan nodded. "But how do we hide from something that hunts by magic?"

Mia looked at her needles, a new idea forming. Her magic was about creation, about weaving. What if she could weave *nothing*?

She pulled out a skein of fine, almost invisible yarn, the kind she used for her most delicate illusions. But this time, she focused on *absence, void, magical nullification*. She began to knit a series of small, shimmering veils, almost imperceptible to the eye, imbued with the power to dampen magical detection.

As she finished each veil, she draped it over herself, Ethan, Queen Sasha, and Bean. The veils settled over them, shimmering faintly, and Mia felt a strange sensation, as if her own magical signature was being muffled, dampened. The air around them felt… empty, devoid of magical presence.

"This should hide our magical signatures," Mia whispered, her voice barely audible. "They won't be able to track us."

They left the ancient path, plunging into the dense, untouched wilderness of the forest. The trees here were even older, their branches forming a thick canopy that blocked out most of the light, plunging them into a perpetual twilight. The ground was uneven, covered in thick moss and tangled roots, making their progress slow and difficult.

They moved silently, carefully, their every step a deliberate act of stealth. Bean, usually so eager to explore, stayed close, her nose twitching, her eyes scanning the shadows. Hopsy, the knitted rabbit, seemed to dim slightly, its internal light flickering, as if its own magical essence was being suppressed by Mia's veils.

They heard the Shadow Hounds enter the forest, their guttural snarls echoing through the trees, growing closer, then receding, then growing closer again. They were searching, sniffing the air, but they seemed disoriented, unable to pinpoint their location. Mia's veils were working.

They walked for hours, pushing through the dense undergrowth, their bodies aching, their minds weary. Queen Sasha, though still weak, showed remarkable resilience, her determination unwavering. She was a queen, and she would not be recaptured.

As night fell, the twin moons rose, casting long, distorted shadows through the thick canopy. The air grew cold, and the pervasive sense of dread returned, stronger now that they were off the path, lost in the ancient, untamed wilderness.

Suddenly, a piercing shriek echoed through the forest, a sound of pure malevolence that sent a chill down Mia's spine. It was followed by a series of guttural roars, and the crashing of branches.

"What was that?" Ethan whispered, his hand on his knife.

Queen Sasha's eyes widened in fear. "The Night Horrors! Creatures of the deepest darkness, drawn to despair and fear. Malakor has unleashed them."

Mia's heart pounded. Night Horrors. She couldn't see them, but she could feel their presence, a cold, predatory aura that permeated the air. Her veils would hide their magical signatures, but not their physical presence. And her magic, though returned, was not for direct combat against such creatures.

"We need light," Mia whispered, her voice trembling. "Something to scare them off."

She pulled out a skein of bright, shimmering gold yarn. She focused on *radiance, warmth, pure light*. Her fingers flew, weaving a delicate, intricate pattern.

She knitted a massive, luminous orb, a sphere of pure, golden light that pulsed with an intense warmth. As she finished, she flung it high into the air.

The orb exploded in a burst of blinding golden light, illuminating the entire section of the forest. The Night Horrors, caught in the sudden brilliance, shrieked, their shadowy forms recoiling, hissing as the light touched them. They were creatures of darkness, and the pure, unadulterated light was anathema to them.

The Night Horrors scattered, their shrieks fading into the distance as they retreated from the light.

"That was amazing, Mia!" Ethan exclaimed, his voice filled with awe.

Mia, panting, felt the drain of the magic, but the warmth in her needles remained, a testament to her growing power. She had faced creatures of darkness, and she had driven them back with light.

They continued their journey, guided by the faint glow of the golden orb, which slowly descended, casting a comforting light on their path. The forest, though still ancient and untamed, felt less menacing under its radiant glow.

As dawn approached, they stumbled upon a hidden clearing. In its center, a massive, ancient oak tree stood, its branches reaching towards the sky like a colossal, living monument. Its bark was scarred with ancient runes, and a faint, ethereal hum emanated from its roots.

"The Heart Tree," Queen Sasha whispered, her voice filled with reverence. "A place of ancient power, a source of light for Solara. It is a waypoint on the ancient path."

Mia felt a strange pull towards the tree, a sense of profound connection. She walked towards it, her hand reaching out to touch its rough bark. As her fingers brushed the ancient wood, a surge of pure, vibrant energy flowed into her, revitalizing her, replenishing her magic. Her needles hummed with a renewed intensity, their warmth spreading through her body, filling her with a sense of boundless power. She felt completely restored, stronger than ever before.

"My magic… it's fully restored," Mia breathed, her eyes wide with wonder. "And more."

Ethan touched the tree, and felt a similar surge of energy, a profound sense of peace. Queen Sasha, too, seemed to draw strength from the ancient tree, her frail form straightening, her eyes shining with renewed hope.

"The Heart Tree recognizes the Weaver," Queen Sasha said, a faint smile gracing her lips. "It offers its strength to those who seek to mend Solara."

They rested at the Heart Tree, allowing its ancient magic to fully restore them. Mia felt a surge of confidence. She was ready. Ready for whatever Malakor could throw at them.

As they prepared to leave, a new sound reached them – the distant, rhythmic thud of hooves, growing closer. The sorcerer's forces. They had found them again.

"He's relentless," Ethan muttered, his hand on his knife.

"Let him come," Mia said, her voice calm, her eyes gleaming with a fierce determination. Her needles hummed with power, ready for battle. "We're not running anymore."

They emerged from the clearing, back onto the ancient path, and waited. The sounds of the approaching forces grew louder, closer. Soon, they would be upon them.

From the shadows of the forest, a wave of shadowy figures emerged – the sorcerer's guards, their dark robes blending with the gloom, their hooked staffs crackling with malevolent energy. And behind them, a chilling sight: two massive Shadow Hounds, their smoky forms swirling, their eyes glowing with cold, malevolent light, their guttural snarls echoing through the trees.

And then, he appeared. Malakor. The dark sorcerer. He stood at the head of his forces, his face still hidden in the depths of his hood, but his aura of immense, malevolent power was palpable, radiating cold and despair.

"The Weaver," Malakor hissed, his voice a dry, rasping sound that seemed to scrape against Mia's soul. "You have defied me for too long. Your petty magic is no match for my power. Solara will fall, and you will be my slave." He raised a hand, and dark energy crackled around his fingertips, coalescing into a sphere of pure shadow.

Mia stepped forward, her rosewood needles clutched in her hands, their warmth a defiant glow against the cold of Malakor's magic. Ethan stood beside her, his stance firm, his eyes fixed on the sorcerer. Queen Sasha, though still frail, stood tall, her gaze unwavering. Bean, at Mia's feet, let out a low, challenging growl. Hopsy, the knitted rabbit, perched on Mia's shoulder, its button eyes glowing faintly.

"Solara will not fall," Mia declared, her voice clear and strong, resonating with the power of the Heart

Tree. "And Queen Sasha will return to her throne. Your darkness ends here, Malakor."

She pulled out a skein of shimmering, iridescent yarn, the kind she used for her most elaborate transformations. She focused, not on a physical object, but on a sensation, an overwhelming sensory overload, a counter to Malakor's oppressive darkness.

"Ethan! Queen Sasha! Get ready!" she yelled.

With a sudden, powerful surge of magic, Mia began to knit. Her fingers flew, a blur of motion, her rosewood needles humming with an almost frantic energy, drawing on the boundless power of the Heart Tree. She poured all her will, all her magic, into the yarn, weaving a grand, dazzling display, a tapestry of pure light and vibrant life.

She knitted a sudden, blinding flash of pure, white light that erupted from her hands, momentarily engulfing the entire forest. The sorcerer and his guards cried out, shielding their eyes, disoriented by the unexpected brilliance. The Shadow Hounds recoiled, howling in pain, their smoky forms flickering, unable to withstand the pure light.

Then, as the light faded, a new creation took hold. The forest seemed to burst into a riot of color and sound. Thousands of glowing, ethereal butterflies, knitted with vibrant, iridescent yarn, fluttered through the air, their wings beating silently, creating a shimmering, living cloud. The air filled with a cacophony of joyful chirps, melodic singing, and the gentle rustle of unseen leaves, a symphony of pure, vibrant life. Flowers of every imaginable hue bloomed instantly on the forest floor, their petals unfurling in slow motion, emitting sweet, intoxicating perfumes. The very ground seemed to pulse with a gentle, rhythmic beat, and the ancient trees shimmered with renewed life.

It was a sensory overload, a full-immersion illusion designed to overwhelm and disorient Malakor and his forces, to counter his darkness with an explosion of pure, unadulterated light and life. The sorcerer and his guards staggered, clutching their heads, their dark magic struggling against the sheer, chaotic power of Mia's creation. They were lost in the illusion, trapped in a vibrant, overwhelming dream of Solara's true essence. The Shadow Hounds howled, their forms flickering, unable to withstand the pure light.

"Now!" Mia yelled, grabbing Ethan's hand.

They dashed forward, through the swirling, vibrant chaos of Mia's creation, towards the ancient path.

Queen Sasha, though still frail, moved with surprising speed, her eyes shining with tears of joy at the sight of Solara's true beauty. Bean, barking excitedly, darted ahead, her tail wagging furiously. Hopsy, the knitted rabbit, seemed to pulse with a joyful light, its button eyes wide with wonder.

They ran, leaving the disoriented sorcerer and his forces behind, lost in the overwhelming beauty of Mia's magic. The ancient path stretched before them, leading them towards the portal, towards home. The threads of their quest, once so tangled and uncertain, were now unraveling, leading them directly to the final act of their impossible adventure.

Chapter 10: The Grand Tapestry and a New Dawn

The vibrant, chaotic beauty of Mia's illusion swirled around them, a dazzling tapestry of light and life that momentarily held Malakor and his forces captive. Thousands of glowing, ethereal butterflies fluttered through the air, their iridescent wings beating silently, creating a shimmering, living cloud. The air filled with a cacophony of joyful chirps, melodic singing, and the gentle rustle of unseen leaves, a symphony of pure, vibrant life. Flowers of every imaginable hue bloomed instantly on the forest floor, their petals unfurling in slow motion, emitting sweet, intoxicating perfumes. The very ground seemed to pulse with a gentle, rhythmic beat, and the ancient trees shimmered with renewed vitality.

"Now!" Mia yelled, her voice hoarse but strong, pulling Ethan's hand.

They dashed forward, through the swirling, vibrant chaos of Mia's creation. Queen Sasha, though still frail, moved with surprising speed, her eyes shining with tears of joy at the sight of Solara's true beauty, a glimpse of her kingdom as it once was. Bean, barking excitedly, darted ahead, her tail wagging furiously, her tiny body vibrating with pure joy.

Hopsy, the knitted rabbit, seemed to pulse with a joyful light, its button eyes wide with wonder, a tiny sentinel of hope.

The illusion was a masterpiece of sensory overload, designed to counter Malakor's oppressive darkness with an explosion of pure, unadulterated light and life. The sorcerer and his guards staggered, clutching their heads, their dark magic struggling against the sheer, chaotic power of Mia's creation. They were lost in the illusion, trapped in a vibrant, overwhelming dream of Solara's true essence. The Shadow Hounds howled, their smoky forms flickering, unable to withstand the pure light, recoiling in pain.

They ran, leaving the disoriented sorcerer and his forces behind, lost in the overwhelming beauty of Mia's magic. The ancient path stretched before them, leading them towards the portal, towards home. The threads of their quest, once so tangled and uncertain, were now unraveling, leading them directly to the final act of their impossible adventure.

The path, though still winding and overgrown, felt different now. The trees seemed to lean in, their ancient branches forming a guiding tunnel, the glowing fungi pulsed with a more welcoming light, and the air hummed with a subtle, familiar energy —

the resonance of the portal. Mia's needles, still warm in her hand, pulsed in sync with the environment, guiding her, urging her onward.

"How much further, Your Majesty?" Ethan asked, his voice strained but hopeful, as he continued to support Queen Sasha.

"Not far, young one," Queen Sasha whispered, her breath coming in ragged gasps, but a growing light in her eyes. "The portal… it lies at the heart of the Whispering Falls. A place of ancient power, where the veil between worlds is thinnest."

They pushed on, driven by the urgency of escape and the promise of a return. Mia, despite the lingering exhaustion, felt a surge of adrenaline. Her magic, fully restored by the Heart Tree, felt boundless, ready for whatever final challenge Malakor might throw at them. She kept a constant awareness of their surroundings, her senses extended, listening for any sign of pursuit.

The illusion, she knew, wouldn't last forever. Malakor was powerful, and his rage would be immense. He would recover, and he would come for them. They had to reach the portal before he did.

The sounds of pursuit began to return, faint at first, then growing steadily louder — the furious shouts of

Malakor, the guttural snarls of the Shadow Hounds, the heavy thud of guards' boots. He was relentless, driven by a desperate need to reclaim his prize and crush the Weaver who dared to defy him.

"He's gaining!" Ethan yelled, glancing over his shoulder. "He's breaking through the illusion!"

Mia's heart pounded. She needed another diversion. Something to buy them more time. She pulled out a skein of dark, earthy brown yarn, the kind she had used for the Mire Beast. She focused on *entanglement, binding, slowing.*

As they ran, she flung the yarn behind them. It landed on the path, instantly sprouting into a dense, thorny tangle of roots and vines, twisting and growing with impossible speed, forming a labyrinthine snare that completely blocked the path. The roots glowed faintly with a malevolent green light, and any attempt to touch them would result in a painful, binding grip.

They heard Malakor's furious roar as he slammed into the new barrier, his dark magic struggling against the magically reinforced roots. The Shadow Hounds howled, trying to tear through the tangle, but the roots held firm, their magic resisting the creatures' attempts.

"That should buy us a few more minutes!" Mia yelled, pushing herself faster.

The ancient path finally opened into a vast, shimmering cavern. The air here was filled with the soft, melodic sound of falling water, echoing off unseen surfaces. And in the center of the cavern, a magnificent sight awaited them.

A colossal waterfall cascaded from a dizzying height, its waters not clear, but a swirling vortex of iridescent light – emeralds, sapphires, and amethysts blending into a liquid rainbow. The water pulsed with a soft, rhythmic beat, and the air around it shimmered with an intense magical energy, a palpable vibration that made the very ground hum. This was the Whispering Falls, and at its heart, the portal.

The portal itself was not a defined archway, but a shimmering, translucent membrane within the waterfall, a swirling vortex of pure light that seemed to beckon them forward. It pulsed with an inviting warmth, a stark contrast to the cold, oppressive magic of Malakor.

"The portal!" Queen Sasha cried, her voice filled with a profound relief, tears streaming down her face. "We are almost there!"

But their moment of triumph was short-lived. Just as they reached the edge of the cavern, a blinding flash of dark energy erupted from the ancient path behind them. Malakor. He had broken through the barrier.

He stood at the entrance to the cavern, his dark robes billowing, his face still hidden in the depths of his hood, but his aura of immense, malevolent power was palpable, radiating cold and despair. Behind him, his remaining guards, battered and bruised, and the two Shadow Hounds, snarling, their smoky forms flickering with rage.

"You will not escape, Weaver!" Malakor hissed, his voice a dry, rasping sound that seemed to scrape against Mia's soul. "Solara is mine! And your magic will be mine!" He raised both hands, and dark energy crackled around his fingertips, coalescing into a massive sphere of pure shadow, growing larger, more menacing.

Mia stepped forward, her rosewood needles clutched in her hands, their warmth a defiant glow against the cold of Malakor's magic. Ethan stood beside her, his stance firm, his eyes fixed on the sorcerer, his hand on his knife. Queen Sasha, though still frail, stood tall, her gaze unwavering, her spirit rekindled by the sight of her home. Bean, at Mia's feet, let out a low, challenging growl. Hopsy, the knitted rabbit, perched on Mia's shoulder, its button eyes glowing faintly, its tiny body vibrating with anticipation.

"Solara will not fall," Mia declared, her voice clear and strong, resonating with the power of the Heart Tree and the ancient magic of the land. "And Queen Sasha will return to her throne. Your darkness ends here, Malakor!"

She pulled out a skein of shimmering, iridescent yarn, the kind she used for her most elaborate transformations, the yarn she had used to create the grand illusion in the forest. But this time, she focused on something more profound: *reversal, unraveling, purification.* She would not just create an illusion; she would unravel his darkness.

"Ethan! Queen Sasha! Get ready!" she yelled, her voice filled with a fierce determination.

With a sudden, powerful surge of magic, Mia began to knit. Her fingers flew, a blur of motion, her rosewood needles humming with an almost frantic energy, drawing on the boundless power of the Heart Tree and the ancient magic of the Whispering Falls. She poured all her will, all her magic, into the yarn, weaving a grand, dazzling display, a tapestry of pure light and vibrant life, but also a force of purification.

As Malakor hurled his sphere of shadow towards them, Mia flung her knitted creation forward. It exploded in a burst of pure, blinding white light that erupted from her hands, meeting Malakor's shadow sphere head-on. The two forces clashed, light against darkness, creation against destruction, in a silent, explosive struggle that filled the cavern with shimmering energy.

Mia's light, imbued with the power of unraveling, began to consume Malakor's shadow. The sphere of darkness rippled, flickered, then began to dissolve, its malevolent energy dissipating into nothingness. Malakor cried out, a sound of pure agony and disbelief, as his power was undone.

Then, as the light faded, Mia's final creation took hold. The cavern seemed to burst into a riot of color and sound, but this time, it was not an illusion. It was Solara's true magic, unleashed. Thousands of glowing, ethereal butterflies, knitted with vibrant, iridescent yarn, fluttered through the air, their wings beating silently, creating a shimmering, living cloud that swirled around Malakor and his forces. The air filled with a cacophony of joyful chirps, melodic singing, and the gentle rustle of unseen leaves, a symphony of pure, vibrant life. Flowers of every imaginable hue bloomed instantly on the cavern floor, their petals unfurling in slow motion, emitting sweet, intoxicating perfumes. The very ground seemed to pulse with a gentle, rhythmic beat, and the ancient stones of the cavern shimmered with renewed life.

Malakor and his guards staggered, clutching their heads, their dark magic struggling against the overwhelming purity of Mia's creation. They were not merely disoriented; they were being *purified*. The light and life of Solara, channeled through Mia's needles, was purging the darkness from them. The Shadow Hounds howled, their smoky forms flickering, then dissolving into wisps of harmless mist, unable to withstand the pure light. The guards, their dark robes fading to a dull gray, collapsed to the ground, their forms still, their malevolence drained.

Malakor himself shrieked, a sound of profound pain and defeat. His dark robes began to unravel, his hood falling back to reveal a face twisted not by evil, but by ancient, profound despair. His body began to shimmer, to dissolve, the darkness that had sustained him being consumed by the pure light of Solara. He was being unmade, unraveled, returned to nothingness. With a final, guttural cry, Malakor vanished, leaving behind only a faint, lingering scent of ozone and the echo of his despair.

The cavern filled with a profound silence, broken only by the gentle murmur of the Whispering Falls and the soft, joyful chirping of Mia's knitted butterflies. The oppressive magic was gone. The darkness had been vanquished.

Mia, panting, leaned on Ethan, her needles still warm in her hand, their hum a steady, triumphant thrum. She had done it. She had defeated Malakor.

Queen Sasha, tears streaming down her face, walked forward, her steps gaining strength with every stride. She knelt beside the fallen guards, and as she touched them, the grayness faded, replaced by the natural hues of their skin and clothing. They were not dead, but merely unconscious, their minds purged of Malakor's dark influence.

"The balance is restored," Queen Sasha whispered, her voice filled with profound gratitude. "The darkness is lifted. Solara is free."

She turned to Mia, her eyes shining with unshed tears. "You are truly the Heart Weaver, Mia Martinez. You have mended the threads of our world, and brought light back to our land."

Suddenly, the cavern entrance filled with figures. Not guards, but people. Solaraians. They were dressed in simple, earthy clothes, their faces etched with worry, but their eyes widened in disbelief and then erupted in joyous cries as they saw their queen, free and standing tall.

"Queen Sasha!" they cried, rushing forward, their voices filled with adoration and relief. They embraced her, weeping, laughing, their joy palpable, contagious. The gloom that had shrouded their faces for so long lifted, replaced by radiant smiles.

The land itself seemed to respond to their joy. The vibrant colors of the cavern intensified, the glowing fungi pulsed with a brighter, more joyous rhythm, and the air filled with a chorus of melodic singing, a symphony of pure, vibrant life that echoed through the cavern. The twin moons outside seemed to shine with an even greater brilliance, their light pouring into the cavern, illuminating the scene of reunion and rebirth.

Mia and Ethan watched, overwhelmed by the sheer emotion of the moment. They had witnessed the suffering of Solara, and now, they were witnessing its rebirth. It was a profound, humbling experience.

Later, as the celebrations began outside the cavern, Queen Sasha approached Mia and Ethan. She was surrounded by her people, who gazed at Mia with reverence and gratitude.

"Mia Martinez, Ethan Morgan," Queen Sasha began, her voice strong and regal, "you have saved Solara. You have faced darkness and brought forth light. We owe you a debt we can never repay." She gestured to the portal, shimmering within the waterfall. "The way home is open to you. But if you choose, Solara welcomes you. You, Weaver, have a place here. A vital role in the mending of our world. And you, loyal companion," she said, turning to Ethan, "your wisdom and courage would be invaluable."

Mia looked at the shimmering portal, then at Ethan. Newark, Arkansas. Their quiet life. The familiar comforts. The mundane. And then she looked at Solara, a land of magic and wonder, a land she had helped to save, a land that needed her. Her needles hummed, a silent invitation to weave a new future.

Ethan squeezed her hand. He knew this was her decision. He had followed her into the unknown, and he would follow her wherever she chose to go next. His life had been irrevocably changed by this adventure, and the thought of returning to a purely logical, non-magical existence felt… dull.

Mia closed her eyes, taking a deep breath, letting the pure, vibrant magic of Solara fill her. She thought of Bear, his sacrifice, his unwavering loyalty. She thought of the Heart Weavers, the ancient lineage she was now a part of. She thought of the joy on Queen Sasha's face, the hope in the eyes of her people.

Her eyes opened, clear and resolute. "Solara needs its Weaver," she said, her voice firm, a profound sense of purpose settling over her. "And I… I want to stay. I want to help mend this world. To weave its future."

Ethan smiled, a wide, genuine smile. "Then I'm staying too. Someone's got to keep track of all the magical yarn." He winked.

Queen Sasha's face broke into a radiant smile. "Welcome home, Weaver. Welcome home, loyal companion."

And so, Mia Martinez and Ethan Morgan, the young couple from Boerne, Texas, who had stumbled into a world of magic and dragons, chose to embrace their new destiny. Mia, the Heart Weaver, began her work, her needles humming with the ancient power of Solara, weaving light and life into the land, helping Queen Sasha restore its balance, its vibrancy, its joy. Ethan, her steadfast companion, her practical anchor, helped her navigate this new world, his engineering mind finding new ways to apply logic to magic, to build a future for Solara.

The land healed. The sapphire trees grew taller, their leaves shimmering with renewed brilliance. The glowing flora bloomed with vibrant intensity. The melodious singing returned to the forests, a constant symphony of joy. The twin moons shone brighter, their combined light illuminating a land reborn.

Mia continued to knit, not just for grand purposes, but for the simple joy of creation. She knitted new creatures for the children of Solara, tiny, animated friends that brought laughter and wonder. She knitted beautiful garments that shimmered and changed, bringing joy and comfort. Her magic, once a secret, was now a celebrated gift, a source of hope and renewal.

And though they sometimes thought of Newark, of their quiet house and the familiar streets, they knew their true home was here, in Solara, a land of magic and wonder, where the threads of reality were woven by the hands of a Weaver from Texas, and where peace and happiness reigned once more. The tapestry of their lives had been rewoven, and it was more beautiful, more vibrant, than they could have ever imagined.